INTERVIEW
WITH THE
ANTICHRIST

INTERVIEW WITH THE ANTICHRIST

HIS

HOUR

HAS

COME

JEFF KINLEY

EMANATE

BOOKS

Published in Nashville, Tennessee, by Emanate Books, an imprint of Thomas Nelson. Emanate Books and Thomas Nelson are registered trademarks of HarperCollins Christian Publishing, Inc.

Thomas Nelson titles may be purchased in bulk for educational, business, fund-raising, or sales promotional use. For information, please e-mail SpecialMarkets@ThomasNelson.com.

Unless otherwise noted, Scripture quotations are taken from New American Standard Bible®. Copyright © 1960, 1962, 1963, 1968, 1971, 1972, 1973, 1975, 1977, 1995 by The Lockman Foundation. Used by permission. (www.Lockman.org)

Scripture quotations marked KJV are from the King James Version. Public domain.

All emphasis in Scripture quotations is the author's own.

ISBN 978-0-7852-2984-1 (eBook)
ISBN 978-0-7852-2983-4 (TP)

Library of Congress Control Number: 2019949914

Printed in the United States of America
20 21 22 23 24 LSC 10 9 8 7 6 5 4 3 2 1

To the one true Christ, whose return is soon and whose reign is sure.

CONTENTS

PREFACE

Antichrist.

What do you really know about him? What would you like to know? Curious? If so, then you're in a good place. The Bible prophesies that a lone individual will arise in the last days and be the catalyst for global change. Scripture describes him as being both delightful and deceptive. Diplomatic, yet diabolical. He will be charismatic and charming, but corrupt to the core. Like a subterranean monster volcano, this man will be beautiful and calm on the surface, but hiding underneath will be a heart from hell. Without warning, he will emerge onto the world stage, rising from the waters of mankind. His persona will marry the charisma of John Kennedy, the mystique of Barack Obama, and the arrogance of Alexander the Great.

And though many kings, conquerors, presidents, and premiers have preceded him, none will rival his raw ambition or success at world domination. They are all amateurs in his shadow. And the whole earth will swoon over him.

If Bible prophecy experts are correct, his arrival could be soon.

He will be an international celebrity—bigger than a rock star, more powerful than a president, and more influential than a Kardashian tweet. And according to the book of Revelation, he will dramatically impact the planet and every person living on it.

But for now, his identity remains obscured. Veiled behind God's prophetic curtain, this principal player in history's end-times narrative waits in the wings for his dramatic entrance.

Intelligent, cunning, and deceptively delusional, this unparalleled opportunist will position himself to be in the right place at the right time. But his true character will eventually be revealed. Exuding egotistical self-adoration and armed with a satanic agenda, he will propagate pure evil like no human before him. And he will crown himself "King of kings and Lord of lords."

But what do we really know about this man? What *can* be known about him? What does the Bible actually say about this nefarious individual? How close might we be to his unveiling? And what difference does it really make in your life today?

This fictional narrative will catapult your mind into a world that hasn't happened . . . *yet*. Upon your arrival, you'll see and hear things you never thought possible. That's because the Bible holds nothing back, but instead reveals "history in advance" through an unfiltered lens. It's raw, rugged, and often shocking, but that's the nature of Revelation.

The story you are about to read is told from the perspective of a young journalist close to the one whom the Bible calls the "beast." He will give you a window into the character of Antichrist and how Scripture's last-days plot *could* unfold. You'll witness Antichrist's transformation into the most evil human in history. This imagined prophetic narrative will also reveal how this coming prince may alter reality and impact mankind.

More than merely entertain you with a suspenseful mystery, however, this speculative account will arouse your prophetic curiosity, whetting your appetite for more solid biblical food on the subject. And you'll find that in the last section of the book.

Antichrist is real, my friend. And he is coming.

But so is Someone else.

Maranatha!

JEFF KINLEY

Dear Marc,

As my closest friend, I am entrusting the attached file to you for safekeeping. These are my thoughts and personal reflections, compiled over the past seven years, and since I can think of no one more trustworthy, I am thus committing them to your care. The file is password protected, but I don't imagine you'll have any trouble getting into it. (Hint: you still remember the name of that girl from communications class, don't you?)

By the time you receive this, I will be on my way to join the president at an undisclosed location. I am filled with anticipation, and persuaded that tomorrow will truly be a day for the ages. Who would have imagined that I, of all people, would secure a front-row seat to history in the making. And I take great comfort in the hope that, in spite of what we've all been through in recent years, this one day could prove to be mankind's most glorious moment. I'm sure, by now, you already know what I'm referring to.

Be safe, my friend.
Julien

CHAPTER ONE

"SOMETHING HAS HAPPENED!"

The 7:24 from Bruxelles Central to Paris was delayed that Saturday morning, and I, for one, was glad. Upon arriving at the train station, my immediate observation was that I had never seen it so full of aspiring travelers, and my presence only added to their ranks. To say I was in a rush to leave Brussels would be a gross understatement, as my itinerary was quite urgent. The early morning text alert disturbing my dormant state contained just a single word:

Come.

Though it had originated from an unknown person, I recognized the country and region code. I knew where I was going, but the only question now was whether I would ever be able to leave Brussels, as multiple routes were experiencing uncommon delays. But my best option remained the Thayls, a high-speed train conceived and built in cooperation with Belgium and France, making travel between our two countries much more convenient and comfortable. At 300 kilometers per hour, station-to-station time between the capital cities was cut to an hour and a half, about the time it takes to check the news over a few coffees and a Danish. However, my journey would not end in Paris, as my final destination was much farther away, in the Middle East.

With no time to properly pack, I had frantically dashed out of my apartment door that morning with not much more than the clothes on my back and my ever-present shoulder bag. Now that I think about it, I can't remember whether I even locked the door. But I suppose that's the kind of behavior you might expect in the midst of crises such as this. And though my twenty-eight-year-old mind had no idea what awaited me upon my arrival, I was quite certain it would be life changing. This was a moment in history, and I was determined to be there . . . and to faithfully record it for future generations.

But before proceeding, perhaps a bit of explanation would be in order here. Allow me to introduce myself. I am Julien De Clercq, a freelance writer, or, more properly, a professional journalist. Following my formal university education in my native Belgium, I officially began pursuing my writing career, completing yearlong internships with two of our most respected news services.

These past three years, however, have seen me engaged in a different sort of writing, the kind that transcends the mere reporting of mainstream news. Put succinctly, I have been tasked with the privilege and responsibility of chronicling the life and career of one individual, a man who has come to be esteemed by all. Of course, it's no secret to whom I am referring. Upon his emergence on the world stage, the now president of the European Alliance of Nations was immediately inundated with requests for television interviews and press conferences. He chose instead a single press event to satiate the media's appetite for information regarding the one who would lead this global coalition.

On the same day of his inauguration, and due to the expediency of the moment, a press conference was held. Hundreds of journalists and reporters from across the world, already in attendance for the inauguration, were invited to this massive news gathering to be held in an auditorium adjacent to the new president's provisional office, located in the heart of Rome. At this time, preparations and construction had not yet been finalized for what later would become his permanent headquarters in Babylon.

At the time, I was in my sixth month of contractual employment at the Belgian Daily Wire (BDW), an independent service based out of Brussels. Our bureau chief had managed to secure me a spot among the sea of reporters who would assemble there in Rome, and I was most grateful for the opportunity. I distinctly remember the auditorium buzzing with chatter that spring afternoon. As the newly elected president ascended the platform, the world's press corps erupted into an almost coordinated, thunderous applause. In my young life, I don't recall ever witnessing such a unified spirit among those whose job it was, not to cheer and affirm politicians, but rather to question and doubt them! Even so, the hurrahs eventually subsided and the meeting began.

Dozens of questions were simultaneously hurled at the man onstage, amid the incessant clicking of camera shutters, whose echoes filled the Roman theater. The president's answers were eloquent, elaborate, and, most of all, convincing. He even managed to inject some humor, prompting laughter throughout the large room. And more applause. I observed that all his responses were given without notes or the conventional aid of a teleprompter. I would later learn that these extemporaneous speaking skills came second nature for this charismatic individual. No matter the question, he fielded them all with the competence of a seasoned orator, as if he had been doing this all his life, which, of course, he had not. His command of multiple languages, his knowledge of geopolitics, and his ability to seamlessly transition from subject to subject were both remarkable and impressive, to say the least.

As a junior journalist, I was assigned a seat approximately two-thirds back in the press corps, not a favorable location for someone aspiring to be recognized by the podium. In the hopes of being noticed in a sea of reporters, I had purposefully chosen to wear my black, yellow, and red-striped tie, representing the colors of the Belgian flag. Perhaps it worked, because to my utter surprise, approximately twenty minutes into the question-and-answer session, the recently sworn-in leader unexpectedly pointed in my direction.

It took a few seconds to determine exactly who he was recognizing, as we all had our hands in the air. But then, with the help of his assistants, I was shocked to discover that he was singling me out in the midst of hundreds! This somewhat confused me, for why should a man as powerful and prominent as him acknowledge someone as small and insignificant as me? Our online readership was modest, and even more so compared to the news giants represented there that day. But in any case, I was thrilled to be the needle he had plucked out of this journalistic haystack.

On the trip down to Rome, I had carefully prewritten five specific questions I deemed relevant and newsworthy for the occasion. Unfortunately, four of the five had already been asked by other reporters, leaving me with my fifth and final question, which had nothing really to do with policy, his cabinet, or the specific makeup of the newly formed alliance. Rather, it was a question much more personal in nature. And so, jumping to my feet and hoping I wouldn't stumble over my words, I cleared my throat.

Unexpectedly, at that very moment, the room's decibel level suddenly fell, as if someone had shut off a running faucet. The verbal traffic came to a complete standstill as the white noise of reporters jockeying for recognition abruptly subsided. I felt for certain the professional journalists gathered there were wondering why someone as obscure as me had been given the opportunity to pose a question to this powerful man at such a critical hour. My peripheral vision caught a jealous stare from Claude Von Spreckelson, the veteran German correspondent.

Why me? I thought. *Why not him?*

Nevertheless, he *had* called on me. And it was my time to speak. Standing almost at attention, I briefly glanced down, past my colorful tie, to my small, dog-eared notepad. Having previously crossed through the first four questions, I now stared at the last one, the least relevant of the five. This made me nervous.

"Yes, sir . . ."

"Speak up!" a voice from the other side of the room barked.

"We can't hear!" another annoyed journalist yelled.

A few snickers rippled through the audience, presumably at me for my lack of readiness and unproven journalistic credentials. Undeterred, I continued, making a second—and louder—attempt this time.

"Yes, sir. I was wondering . . . er . . . what I mean is . . ."

The man behind the podium leaned forward, his brow furrowed slightly. "Well, go ahead. Get on with it. Spit it out, young man."

And so, that's exactly what I did.

"Why *you*, sir?" I inquired.

It felt good to say it. To get it out. To be *heard*. I enjoyed a certain degree of satisfaction to be able to ask my question at such a momentous meeting. But the asking was only half the moment's drama. What I really wondered was, how would he respond to my peculiar inquiry?

The president's head tilted slightly, and a faint puzzled expression emerged on his face. This unexpected response prompted me to elaborate.

"Precisely, Mr. President, what I mean to say is, why do you believe you are the most suited person for this position? Why are you the right man for this unprecedented moment in history?"

A minor surge of self-confidence accompanied my words, having amplified and clarified my original question.

Upon hearing my explanation, his expression immediately transitioned, and a smile peeked from the corner of his mouth.

Looking back, I now credit that single question with officially launching my journalistic career in full force.

He responded, "Excellent question, young man." He then answered with a swagger, his words rehearsing for all of us, and a watching world, six itemized reasons why *he*, and none other, could bring calm to our chaos and put the nations back on the road to peace and prosperity. The world's press corps seemed stimulated by his words, and following several more rounds of questions, the conference was dismissed to deafening applause. By all accounts, most there that day seemed to believe there was actually hope for the future. And that this man would be able to deliver it. The president seemed pleased as well—smiling, waving, and shaking hands as he exited the theater.

While shuffling out of the room, I received several approving nods from older journalists, as if to say, "Nice going, kid." I remember thinking that this would be the highlight of my career, something I would be able to build upon, as my face and voice had been broadcast all over the world. However, something quite unexpected happened to me as I was leaving the theater. A man approached me, identifying himself as a representative of the president's security team. He informed me that I had been invited to personally meet with the president on the following day. As I was unprepared for the moment, I found myself hesitating, explaining how eager I was to get back to Brussels and that I was presently on my way to the airport for the return flight later that evening. He didn't even acknowledge my comment, but rather informed me that my flight would be changed, a room would be booked for the night, and all my expenses were covered for the extra day's stay.

"Oh. Okay. Well, in that case, great!" was all I could muster, gladly accepting the invite.

The next morning, after only a few hours' sleep, there was a knock at my hotel door. I scurried to grab my things, then accompanied an aide downstairs to an awaiting car, which then carried me to the new administration's temporary offices downtown. I was led into a marble-lined room with a sitting area. It was decorated with two luxurious couches and equally fashionable chairs, with a table between them, upon which was a coffee carafe with two cups on a silver tray. I was asked to sit and told that the president would join me shortly.

As I waited, my eyes scanned the walls, where I observed several museum-worthy paintings, on which were depicted various religious and military scenes and personalities. One of them especially commanded my attention. I took a picture of it, later researching it online. Turns out it's a work by Nicolas Poussin, painted in 1638, titled *The Conquest of Jerusalem by Emperor Titus*, the first-century Roman general. I stood up and strolled over to get a closer look, admiring the detail and depth of such a work of art. Just then, the door opened, and the president walked in, accompanied by a small entourage.

Observing my keen interest in the painting, he explained, "It's an original, in case you were wondering. On loan to us from the Vienna Gallery, where it has hung since 1721."

"It's very impressive, sir."

"Yes, it is," he replied. "I like it because it depicts the glory that was once Rome."

He motioned for me to sit on the sofa, which was adjacent to the oversized wingback chair he soon occupied. No formal introductions were necessary. He knew who I was and I certainly knew who he was. His suit, shirt, and tie were immaculate, and he was taller than I expected. On his lapel he wore a pin with ten white stars against a sky blue background. A larger, gold star was prominently displayed in the center.

During what proved to be only a ten-minute meeting, I remained convinced he could detect how nervous I was.

He began. "Mr. De Clercq"—his tone was direct, and it was clear he would dispense with small talk—"your question at yesterday's press gathering was . . . well, *unexpected*."

I managed a nervous smile. "Yes, Mr. President. I suppose it was, sir. You see, my other questions had already been—"

"You went right for the heart of the matter, and that is something I can truly appreciate." His sober interruption silenced me. I would later learn this to be his style. In any conversation, his would be the predominant voice. Settling more comfortably into the large chair, he continued.

"This is a dark hour in which we find ourselves, Mr. De Clercq. Trust in leadership right now, on a global scale, is at a historic low, and yet this trust is paramount to our cause. Without it, nothing can be accomplished. As I told you yesterday in my response to your question, I believe destiny chooses the man, not the other way around." He paused. "I was born for this moment. I *know* it."

The man sitting across from me exuded an inherent assuredness. It was his natural scent. He was resolute and determined. Charming, yes. Yet simultaneously intimidating. I could sense he wanted something from me. And I was right.

"But the question here, right now, is, 'Were *you*?'"

I was caught off guard, not catching his meaning. My mind and attention were being pulled in several directions as I reminded myself I was in a room with arguably the most important and powerful man in the world. His presence was ambient, setting the tone and temperature of the meeting. And sitting within arm's length of him, I could feel his persuasiveness encroaching on my will. It was as if I were all alone with him, though his secretary and advisors were also present, along with a personal bodyguard so huge I was convinced he ate people like me for breakfast.

I heard myself say, "Was I *what*, sir . . . Mr. President?"

He shot back without hesitation. "Why, *born* for this moment, of course! Are you the kind of man who believes in destiny, or just one of billions who ramble aimlessly from home to work each day? Born one day and die the next. What life is that? What I want to know is whether you are the kind of journalist and writer who is merely reporting the news as he sees it . . . or one who hungers for a *real* story to tell, one for the ages?"

He lifted one eyebrow, adding, "Put another way, De Clercq, when you leave here today and return to your little Belgian cubicle to trade a seven-hundred-word article for a few euros—will you be content with that? Or does something within you long for more?"

He edged forward in his chair, and closer toward me. His eyes fixated upon mine, and with all the sincerity of a marriage proposal, he asked, "Julien, would you like to step into history with me?"

Frankly, I had no clue what he was talking about.

"*Step into history*, sir? I'm afraid I'm a bit lost here."

He leaned back and laughed. "You see," he said, turning to his staff, "that's what I like about this young man. He's a journalist without a preconceived agenda. A rare find indeed."

Then, turning his attention back toward me, he elaborated. "De Clercq, I detect a genuineness in you. You're authentic, fresh, and untainted by the bitterness that has characterized so much of the press these past few decades."

He glanced down at my shoulder bag on the floor beside my chair.

"I see you have one of my campaign buttons on your bag. It helps that you're already a fan, or at least convinced enough to vote for me, I presume. In some ways, you actually remind me of *me*," he said, laughing a second time. "You are enthusiastic, inquisitive, and with, I suspect, a hidden ambition just waiting for the chance to be unleashed."

I had forgotten about the button, and I felt a bit embarrassed that he had noticed it.

"Okay then, let me put it plainly to you . . . just as you were straightforward with me yesterday," he added, stroking his chin. He took a slow breath, then exhaled and said, "De Clercq, I want you to consider becoming my official biographer."

I felt the blood instantly rush from my face, and I feared I would either faint or vomit on the Persian rug beneath my feet. I'm certain my pallid condition was obvious to all present, evidenced by the smile that broke across the president's face. I also heard a faint snicker from behind me.

This was an offer, no, *the* offer of a lifetime. Of *ten* lifetimes. Any writer wouldn't hesitate to jump at the chance to etch himself or herself into history's archives this way. They say your whole life flashes before your eyes just before dying, but in that few seconds' pause, my mind instead raced *forward* in time. Such a rare open door would allow a young writer like me the privilege of being catapulted into literary recognition and prominence.

I envisioned transitioning from a struggling, small-time online reporter to achieving the prestige of chronicling the life and political career of one who could quite possibly prove to lift the world out of her current quagmire. From all indications, this man was going to be around for quite some time, leading a new empire and leaving a legacy unlike any who had come before him. So obviously, job security would be another huge plus, with multiple opportunities to follow. I would never want for a paycheck again. I could replace my old laptop. And I would certainly be able to move out of that one-bedroom dump I presently called home.

All these thoughts simultaneously swirled around in my brain as I contemplated this unique and unusual proposal. At the same time, I also found myself deeply humbled, and again wondered, *Why me?*

I stared into space for what couldn't have been more than a few seconds. Then, regaining my composure, I turned my attention back to the president and began slowly nodding. "Yes, sir! *Yes, sir!*" I said. "Of course. I would be honored. It would be a pleasure to serve you in this way. Whatever you need, I'll do it!"

His grin widened. "Excellent. Then we're all set. My team has already fully vetted you, and your background check has cleared security protocol. You also come from good stock, De Clercq. A good family. In fact, my team tells me your mother makes the best *pain à la Grecque* in all of Brussels."

To this day, I don't know how he could have known that. But at the moment, it didn't matter much to me.

"It's settled, then," he announced, standing to his feet. "We will set up an interview schedule and get you started right away."

He extended his hand toward me, and I snapped to my feet, suddenly aware of how underdressed I was for a meeting with a world leader. I reached forward to give him a firm handshake. And while our hands remained clasped, his smile momentarily disappeared. "Julien," he said, lowering his voice, "this is an assignment unlike anything you've ever done. As such, you need to know that confidentiality is of the upmost importance. Some of what I reveal and what you observe will, by necessity, be kept from the public eye until after it has been declassified. I don't have to tell you that any information leak or breach of trust will result in immediate termination, no questions asked. There can be no foul-ups or failures here. Are we clear?"

"Of course. I understand. You can count on me, Mr. President. I won't let you down."

"Perfect," he replied, giving my hand one final shake. "My staff will contact you with the necessary security clearance arrangements and confidentiality documents you'll need to sign." And with a confirming glance at his staff, he concluded, "So, until I see you again, Julien De Clercq, be at peace . . . and be safe!"

And with that, he was whisked out of the room by his secretary and security detail, staff in tow. I was left alone, save for the agent whose job it was to transport me to the airport for my flight home. He smiled at me, raising an eyebrow and slowly shaking his head.

"Do you have any idea what just happened here? What just happened to *you*?" he said. "You're one of the luckiest young men on the planet right now. And my advice to you is, enjoy it while you can. And don't screw up," he added. "The president is a good and fair man, but he doesn't suffer fools, and has little tolerance for incompetence. Do your job and do it well, and you *will* be rewarded."

I nodded. "Thank you. I will do my best."

Though that was more than three years ago, it still plays like a fresh imprint in my memory.

• • •

A loud tone sounded, and the female voice on the station's public address system finally announced the departure of my train. Traffic in Brussels was gridlocked, with several main arteries leading in and out of the city grinding to a halt on that Saturday morning. Even finding a seat on a bus proved difficult. Fortunately, I was able to secure transport by sharing a taxi with a neighborhood acquaintance, as he was also on his way downtown. It seemed as if everyone wanted to get out of the city. Some, no doubt, were commuting for business, while others were simply leaving to visit Paris, or perhaps meet up with friends or relatives there.

But this morning's summons to the city of Babylon was not a routine visit for another round of interviews or research. Though the actual reason for my trip was initially unknown, the one-word text I had received would soon be fully explained. In fact, it became abundantly clear the moment I climbed into that taxi.

"Something has happened!" my neighbor announced.

This made me regret taking a sleeping pill and retiring early the previous night. It seemed everyone knew but me. It was written on the cab driver's face. And I suspected it had something to do with why the rail system was running behind schedule. For it was broadcast on every radio station and banner flashed across every screen in the Bruxelles Central Station. Words I never thought I would read.

THE PRESIDENT IS DEAD

CHAPTER TWO

THE VILLA

The station monitors indicated that the 7:24 train was finally ready for boarding. I jockeyed my way through a throng of travelers and up the stairs to platform 5. Climbing aboard the train, I found the first-class comfort section, having been forced there because there were no other seats left. I pulled out my phone and attempted a call to my contact in the president's office. No answer. Again, I lamented going to bed early the previous night, as I felt so in the dark regarding the news.

The train quickly filled with passengers, and within minutes we were Paris bound. The onboard Wi-Fi was unreliable and slow that particular day, making news reports erratic. Not that it would have mattered anyway, as what was reported didn't reveal much. But what virtually every traveler on that train did gather from their phones was that there had been an attempt on the president's life following a local dinner engagement just two miles from his Babylon headquarters.

The assailant had used some sort of knife or sword in the attack, fatally wounding the president in the head. The man was instantly

INTERVIEW WITH THE ANTICHRIST

swarmed by security and was shot and killed in the ensuing scuffle. The president was rushed to an undisclosed medical facility, where doctors and surgeons made a valiant attempt to save his life. But the wound proved too severe. And this was the extent of the information playing on a loop on virtually every news source available.

I managed to get through to my old boss back at the Belgian Daily Wire to see if he had any further information on the story, but he informed me his sources could only confirm what the rest of the world was hearing. Babylon was being very tight-lipped about the whole affair. And rightly so, I suppose. In a crisis such as this, rumors, conspiracies, and misinformation are common aftershocks. And the last thing we needed was to report misinformation or to grossly exaggerate reliable facts, misinterpreting them.

I turned around and gazed down the rows of seats and into the train car behind me. Most people were fixated on their phones, making calls or searching for more information. Some simply stared out the window, while others wept silently. This disturbing news had sent the world into a collective state of shock, evidenced in microcosm by the somber spirits of those traveling on the 7:24 that morning. And not surprisingly so, for this president had single-handedly done so much to bring the world back from the brink of collapse.

Outside my window, the picturesque Belgian countryside seemed tranquil and unaffected by the day's news. I closed my eyes, listening to the hum of the train, and reminiscing about earlier, more hopeful times, specifically my first official interview with the president.

Having been vetted and granted official level B security credentials, I was invited to join the president at a private coastal villa located approximately thirty-five kilometers from central Rome.

Before moving into his permanent Babylonian residence, the president would spend many weekends at this villa, a welcomed relief from the ever-increasing pressures and demands of political life. It was here, just one week after my first meeting with him, that I conducted my inaugural interview.

Among its many amenities, the 1903 Italian mansion boasted seven bedrooms, a pool, an office, and a half-hectare (approximately one acre) rear garden area with a meticulously manicured lawn and sculptured shrubs. And all this overlooked the beautiful Tyrrhenian Sea. Upon my arrival, I was led through the manor and out into the back garden, where I immediately spotted the president seated at a glass-topped, rectangular table. A large, white canopied umbrella provided cover from the sun. The president's dress was considerably more casual than the last time we had met. His white open-collared shirt and Mediterranean-blue poplin trousers gave him more the look of a yacht owner than an international government head.

He recognized me, signaling me to come to him.

"Young Julien, how good it is to see you again. Come. Sit with me."

An aide pulled a chair for me opposite him. I slid my brown satchel off my shoulder and sat down.

"I trust your flight was uneventful and that the accommodations here will prove suitable."

"Oh, yes, Mr. President," I replied, looking around at the postcard scenery surrounding me. "No problem getting here. Your staff have been more than gracious. And I have no doubt that my stay will be delightful."

He gave me a reassuring nod, taking a sip from his glass.

"Brandy?" he offered.

"I'm fine, sir. Thank you just the same," I replied.

"Nonsense. You'll have a drink with me. I've recently been given a rare cask of Rémy Martin Louis XIII, and to my delight, this particular cognac is among the finest I've had. There's a flavor of autumn in it, along with a hint of dried fruit and nuts. It's simply the taste of perfection."

He raised his glass again, sniffing it, while snapping his fingers with the other.

"Trevor, bring Mr. De Clercq a brandy," he ordered.

I gratefully acknowledged his provision.

"Should you ever want material pleasures and possessions, I highly recommend getting yourself elected president." He chuckled. "It seems as if everyone, from billionaires to kings, wants to lavish the Alliance leader with gifts. I suppose it's typical in the early days of my administration to receive goodwill from well-wishers, but if the gifts don't stop, we're going to have to build a storehouse for them! You don't, by any chance, have need of a vintage 1966 Harley-Davidson FLH Electra Glide motorcycle, do you, De Clercq?"

I chuckled. "No, sir. I don't believe I do."

"I wouldn't think you would," the president laughed. He savored another sip of his drink, then abruptly changed subjects.

"Okay, so where shall we begin, Julien? This moment marks the beginning of what I trust will be a memorable journey."

I had spent the previous week in feverish preparation, filling nearly half a notebook with questions and follow-ups. However, I thought it best to start by asking the president about what he thought had helped precipitate his meteoric rise to prominence.

"Sir, here we are in the spring, enjoying the beauty and tranquility of this magnificent place. But if you will, take me back to last fall, and the event that stirred you to step forward and take action."

"Yes, of course," he replied, nodding in agreement. He paused, as if holding his breath, then exhaled. His previous joviality disappeared.

I pressed the record button on my digital recorder and opened my leather-encased notepad.

"I still have difficulty comprehending such a mysterious incident. Nothing like it in history, De Clercq. Nothing. At. All. A completely unexpected and unprecedented anomaly. Millions worldwide just vanishing from existence . . . and they are still calculating the losses, and the sheer numbers involved in this tragedy that blindsided the world. It's staggering, really."

"And your *personal* theory or explanation as to what could have caused such a thing?" I interjected.

"We'll get to that. But first, let us consider for a moment the *context* of the days, weeks, and months that followed and how it set in motion my emergence upon the global stage. It is imperative that we recall what it felt like during that awful time. There isn't a person alive today who could not tell you where they were and what they were doing when they heard the awful news. Many even witnessed it firsthand. It goes without saying that this thing has become a defining moment of our generation—in my opinion much more so than past shocking historical events, which indelibly marked humanity—Pearl Harbor, Hiroshima, the Kennedy assassination, 9/11, the 2023 Paris bombings, and so on."

He nursed a sip of brandy, then went on. "You see, Julien, part of what makes happenings such as this so catastrophic and devastating is that, well, there are no warnings. No precursors or ominous clouds of doom riding ahead of them. And certainly no precedents . . . at least for something like this. So, tell me, how could the world have possibly prepared itself? One moment, more than 100 million people are here, and in the blink of an eye, they were not. It happened so suddenly. And that's when panic and disaster struck us all like an unforeseen tsunami. Terror gripped our planet in most areas, especially in Western nations, like the United States. That former superpower was devastated in a single day, not so much from the sheer numbers among their missing, but more so due to the multiple facets of American society that were gutted at every level.

"Around the world, family members were abandoned, and homes left empty. Possessions and money suddenly left unguarded. World commerce ground to a halt. Stock markets crashed. Mortgages went into default. The banking industry collapsed. Global communication networks were overrun and jammed. Children were left without parents and parents without children. Spouses and partners found themselves suddenly abandoned. Why, the immediate fallout on the family unit alone generated an international crisis. Even now, months later, millions worldwide remain orphaned and left without their loved ones."

He shook his head while circling the top of his glass with his finger.

"You know, Julien, I remember as a young boy, when a schoolmate of mine went missing. Our entire community was traumatized for weeks as the search went on and on. Hundreds banded together, vowing to find the little boy, combing the countryside, valleys, and streams. Fear gripped every home. No one knew if he had fallen down a well, drowned in a lake, or been kidnapped by a passing motorist. But you know what?" he said, elevating an eyebrow. "They never found him. To this day, no one knows what happened to him. Or if they do, they're not saying. It was as if he simply *dematerialized*. He just ceased to *be*."

"That's a heartbreaking story, sir."

"Yes, it is. In this case, however, we're not talking about the single abduction of a little boy, are we? What we felt in my little town has been exponentially magnified. The combined world grief brought on by last fall's phenomenon was unbearable . . . still is for some."

My recorder sat on the table, right beside the tulip-shaped glass of brandy that had just been delivered. I left it alone, and the president went on.

"And that's just the tip of the iceberg. There was, as you recall, mass panic in the streets, seen predominantly in metropolitan areas. The suicide rate spiked for weeks, with thousands taking their own lives—shooting themselves, overdosing on narcotics, and jumping out of high-rise windows and off bridges. Local, state, and federal government agencies everywhere became a frenzy of confusion. In some countries, even the armed forces were deeply weakened as a result of losing soldiers and high-ranking officers and commanders. Military radar stations and outposts were left unguarded. There were massive, spur-of-the-moment reorganization and reassignments in the chain of command. The threat of war and invasion was heightened, and military conflict seemed imminent, sending even more shockwaves of dread and hysteria from country to country.

"Several nations lost top governmental leaders and key cabinet members. Patients died on operating tables due to surgeons and nurses disappearing. Many more patients suffered and died in hospitals from neglect. Emergency rooms swelled to overflow capacity, and those injured from automobile accidents related to the global event perished in hospital hallways and parking lots waiting for care. Pilotless commercial airliners plummeted to the ground, killing thousands more. Airport . . . um . . . what do you call those who direct the planes?"

"Air traffic controllers, sir?"

"Right. The air traffic controllers were not able to control or manage the sudden number of requests for emergency landings as passengers vanished from their seats in midflight. This created havoc on board flights, resulting in physical altercations with flight attendants, and some passengers even attempting to storm the cockpit area. And unless failsafe measures had been promptly enacted, nuclear power plants, like the one in Antwerp, just north of your home, could have suffered meltdowns. In my opinion, the failure to reach an agreement years ago to shut down those facilities was a grave error. Even now, you Belgians are still dependent on nuclear power for the majority of your electricity.

"However, what we discovered as a result of that mysterious and fateful day was that we, as nations, as a race of humans, are much more fragile than we care to admit. We exist atop a precarious evolutionary perch, and are easily toppled by crisis. And *that*, my young friend, is precisely why the world desperately needs strong, resolute leadership . . . now, more than ever."

Trevor appeared again, refilling the president's glass. Seeing mine had yet to be touched, he raised an eyebrow, then retreated back into the confines of the villa. The immediate openness the president demonstrated toward me made me secretly wonder if brandy shouldn't be a part of *all* our interviews together. I kept prompting him.

"You were saying, sir?"

"Of course, you already know all this, Julien. You lived through it as I did."

"Yes, sir. However, part of what we're doing here is putting these historical events in your own words, as *you* see them. This is your story, Mr. President. Not merely the reporting of commonly known news or past history."

"Yes. Yes, I see. *My* story."

"Exactly," I replied.

"All right, then. The event and the ensuing chaos. And next, as you recall, was the crime epidemic that hit like an earthquake aftershock. Stores and businesses worldwide were left unattended, becoming open targets for looters. Law enforcement officers found it nearly impossible to address such widespread lawlessness. There was just too much of it in every place. This further led to an outbreak of arson, along with a shortage of food and gas in many areas, including first world nations. The freight industry was unable to meet the demand for food products and necessary resources. And this sent millions into even greater panic, desperation, and insanity, expressing their agony and outrage through riots, shootings, and even bombings of some government buildings."

He took another sip, then furrowed his brow in disapproval.

I privately wished he would begin transitioning from the *world's* story and get on with his own. But I understood his original point regarding the global context of his rise to power. And I didn't want to make a habit of interrupting him.

"Yes, it is all about context, Julien," he repeated.

That's alarming, I thought. *Was this rare brandy enabling him to read my thoughts? Nonsense, Julien. He's still talking. Write!* I scolded myself.

"It's abundantly clear to me that this horrible, unfortunate incident was the worst thing that could have happened to humankind. It awakened something within us that is sinister and dark. Something evil and destructive.

"Although," he remarked with a shoulder shrug, "I suppose it *could* be argued that, in retrospect, things have turned out for the better, globally speaking. With the collapse and implosion of countries like the United States and others, this mass disappearance has actually served to help bring the nations together. And that's positive. Unlike before, today we actually need one another for survival. Nationalism effectively died last fall. It's a failed, fossilized philosophy that has no place in this new world. Globalism has been birthed in its place, and it's working.

"But this grand idea of uniting the world is not new, you know. It has been in formation for more than a century, dating back to the old League of Nations following World War I. Then came the United Nations, followed by the European Economic Community in 1957. But we can talk more about that in a future session. Suffice it to say that many have previously promoted and pushed for a more unified world government, but the times in which we now live *demand* it. As a result, you could say this is actually an exciting era of history!"

His passion and voice rose as the blinding afternoon sun began to set, casting its rays directly toward my line of sight, forcing me to adjust my chair accordingly. I inadvertently placed the sun directly behind the president's head, its orange glow producing a "halo effect" around him, temporarily veiling his face. It dawned on me that this man was occupying his current leadership position by no mere accident or stroke of blind luck. The sun's brilliance behind him seemed emblematic of his personal radiance and political savvy. He was indeed a luminary for our time. A light shining in a dark world.

A tray of neatly arranged cheeses, meat, and fish appeared. "Enjoy" was Trevor's only word before vanishing once again. Garden lights came on, brightening the path leading into the villa.

For the first time since my arrival, I felt comfortable enough to partake, which I did, choosing a selection of meat and cheese for my small plate. The president did the same.

"So," I continued, looking at my notes. "I suppose the proverbial elephant in the room regarding this topic is what actually happened on that fall morning. What I mean to say, sir . . . back to my original question, is, what is your explanation for this sudden departure of so many?"

It was clear to me now how this event had formed the foundation of his sudden acceleration to international prominence.

He chuckled. "*Departure*, huh? You make it sound like they went somewhere, when in fact we simply don't know, do we?"

"No, sir, we don't, but—"

"I hear what you're saying, De Clercq. So, you want to know what *I* think, right? *My* theory?"

"Yes, sir. Of course."

"Well, opinions concerning the matter are as varied and as numerable as those who have them. Every person has his or her own ideas, including a multitude of experts in fields ranging from science to astronomy, philosophy, and even theology. I suppose each of them must be entertained and given their proper due. There are, of course, those who subscribe to the theory that an alien abduction of some sort took place. Some argue that an advanced life form from another galaxy traveled to earth and snatched away millions, however, I find this ironic, given that previously these same people did not believe in life on other planets! How they would ascertain this information or prove their hypothesis is beyond me. Nevertheless, it is theorized that the aliens did this to 'enlighten' the abducted, whereupon one day they will eventually return to earth to convince the rest of us that aliens do indeed exist.

"This, of course, sounds futile and far-fetched to me. More science fiction than science. To my knowledge, there has been no factual or conclusive evidence to support such a preposterous assertion. I mean, in an age where every person carries a camera in their hand at all times, why didn't one, even one person among eight billion, snap a photo of this event? Why no CCTV footage or pictures of extraterrestrial spacecrafts hovering all over the planet, waiting to beam up these poor souls? Don't get me wrong. I believe there could be intelligent life out there. But advanced alien technology that makes millions simply disappear? I would have to drink a lot more before entertaining such an idea."

We both laughed, and he took another piece of cheese from his plate and placed it in his mouth. He chewed thoughtfully, then swallowed before continuing.

"And why would aliens target only *those* people? Why wouldn't larger concentrations of them be taken in other areas, countries, and cities? Why were there parts of the world where the loss was reported as very minimal? Why were countries like Albania and Afghanistan relatively unaffected? Why wasn't I taken as well? Or you?"

Shaking his head in denial, the Alliance's leader argued, "No. I don't buy it. Doesn't sound plausible from an astrophysical perspective."

I momentarily put my pen down to reach for another slice of cheese, noting the declining battery life on my digital recorder. The president didn't notice.

"Now, we know there *are* atmospheric aberrations that can occur, especially in light of recent deteriorating patterns in climate change," he mused. "I am no authority in that field, but those who are have postulated that some irregularities in atmospheric changes *can* lead to deadly concentrations of random, harmful geo-spots, which have been known to prove fatal. Perhaps similar to spontaneous combustion and the like. I realize that explanation doesn't fully explain this phenomenon, but some variation of it could, I repeat, *could* account for what occurred.

"Of course, if you believe in some sort of universal consciousness out there, as many do, you might propose that those millions were removed because they no longer 'fit' with the rest of us—that they weren't earth-friendly, or willing to move toward a global collective consciousness and a unified planet. Again, unprovable.

"Another theory suggests there was a cosmic crack in our universe's space-time continuum, and that some kind of portal was opened to an alternate reality or distant dimension. These people, for reasons unknown, fell into that crack and were essentially swallowed up by the universe. But that plays better in a futuristic fantasy movie than it does in real life.

"Now, the Christian religion also contains a sect that believes in their own version of abduction, this one by God himself. This strikes me as bizarre, especially in light of the fact that many, if not most, others who claim to worship the same God don't hold to such a belief . . . and they're still here with us!

"Others in a more progressive contingency also attribute this removal of millions to an act of God, only it being one of judgment, removing those who were intolerant, hateful, and bigoted. I am no theologian, but to me, *God*, if he does exist, would never do such a thing. Not a good God anyway. Sounds too dark and cruel.

"And again I ask, where is the evidence? We have evolved over millions of years into rational, intelligent beings who require evidentiary documentation for unparalleled occurrences like this. We need more than unfounded theories and religious fairy tales. We need *proof* . . . and though a conclusive explanation has yet to be verified, it is my opinion that an answer will come . . . eventually. And maybe sooner than later. Time will tell. Mankind eventually rises to understand these things. We always do. We were meant to. Look: we've split the atom, healed diseases, traveled to the moon, and sent probes into space, exposing ourselves to an infinite amount of data. We know why earthquakes occur and why weather patterns form. We've mapped the ocean floor and meticulously researched and analyzed virtually every part of the human body. Consider the invention of the MRI machine, DNA mapping, and genetic coding.

"So, yes, in time, it will all become clear," he emphatically restated.

"Truth be known, when it's all said and done, we may not even be surprised at how simple the explanation to this mysterious mass exodus is. The explanation may have been right under our noses all along. Or it could be staring us in the eyes, but we just don't see it yet. But we'll find the answer. History teaches us that there is almost nothing we cannot achieve if we are willing to work together toward a common goal . . . Do you believe that, Julien?"

"Oh, without a doubt, sir. No limits to what we can do if we are willing to be united."

"I like that," he remarked, approvingly. "Well said!"

Another ounce of brandy drained from his glass.

"And so, circling back to our original starting point, sir. Do you believe all this was the genesis of your rise to political prominence?" I asked.

"I suppose you could state it that way, even though I think I would have eventually found my way to this place in leadership regardless. But I'll consent to that. I am much more, however, than the 'opportunist' rival leaders have accused me of being."

He leaned forward in his chair, slowly pushing the meat-and-cheese tray aside.

"Julien, this is not just a job to me. I previously told you that I am *called* to this role and moment in time. It's difficult to explain, but when I saw what was happening to my world, something awoke within me. Something that, as far as I know, may have been lying dormant deep inside all my life. It's as if I was standing at a station platform, waiting for my train to arrive. I just didn't know it would arrive in the form of such an international crisis and catastrophe. But I have successfully brought order out of chaos. Peace in the midst of panic. And I will continue to do so. The European Alliance of Nations will lead the world and effectively transition the human race into a new age.

"Coming together for a common purpose and mutual good is no longer some futuristic, noble ideal. It has now become critical and essential to moving forward as a planet. It's what we *must* do. And it's what we *will* do under my leadership. That's my mission as president, to lead the nations forward toward a bright horizon. Others before me in history have failed in this endeavor," he firmly declared. "I will not."

It was evident he believed every word he was speaking. This was no campaign speech or political rhetoric. These were words from the heart. From the *soul*.

And with that, my digital recorder's low-battery light illuminated.

The president's eyes diverted to his left, as an aide appeared under the archway leading into the villa.

"Well," he concluded. "I suppose that will be enough for now." He stood to shake my hand. "You know, Shakespeare was right, 'the past *is* prologue.' What has already occurred is merely the introduction for what is to come. And great things *are* coming. And on that note, matters of state are calling, and I must go. You'll be contacted regarding our next meeting, which I hope will be soon. Until then, peace and safety to you, young De Clercq."

"Peace and safety to you as well, Mr. President," I responded.

He walked briskly toward his aide, and they both disappeared through the darkened doorway. The sun was almost gone, and the shadows were long on the manicured lawn. I wasn't sure if the growling in my stomach was hunger or anxiety as I contemplated the weight of the task I had been given. For a moment, I felt overwhelmed. The last rays of the setting sun shone through the glass that sat untouched before me during the length of my interview. I reached out and grabbed it, emptying its contents down my throat with a generous swig.

CHAPTER THREE

THE MYSTERY
MAN REVEALED

There was a small snack service on my train, and I made my way forward to secure a cup of coffee. Returning to my seat, I stared at the blurring landscape racing by. In just under ninety minutes, I will be pulling in to the Paris Nord station, after which I will secure a taxi to de Gaulle for my eventual flight to Babylon. After getting dressed earlier that morning, booking a flight was the first thing I did before getting the taxi. I was fortunate to still find an available flight at this late hour. The news of the president's death had spiked travel, as the whole world seemed to be converging upon the political capital. But despite the city's newly elevated status, there was still no direct flight from Brussels to Babylon. There is, however, one from Paris to Baghdad. Therefore, the Thalys proved the quickest way to get me to the next stop on my destination.

The train actually is quite fast. And economical. I sometimes think about how the older generation marvels at the technology that we take for granted today. From artificial intelligence to self-automated vehicles, space drones, free internet worldwide, self-driving trucks, bioprosthetics, the advances mankind has made in the last thirty years have been amazing. Developments in rail transportation alone are enough to astound those old enough to remember the days of conventional travel by road, rail, and air. And there is ongoing testing for the Hyperloop system of train travel, with speeds of up to more than 1,200 kilometers per hour (760 miles per hour) through an oversized vacuum tube. In today's world, speed is key.

Just before she passed away, my grandmother rode on a high-speed train to Austria. What once took six hours in her day has been reduced to just under a two-hour journey. Upon her arrival, she repeatedly asked my mother, "How did we get here so quickly? I don't understand!"

Time is like that. Fleeting. Always running. And frequently deceptive. I think about my own brief life and often wonder the same thing—*How did I get here . . . and so quickly?* It's a question not too dissimilar to the one I posed to the president at the start of our second official interview session, which took place not long before our permanent move to his operational base at Babylon. In contrast to the relaxed villa atmosphere of my initial interview, this one was scheduled to take place over two days at the provisional office facility in central Rome. Instead of a gentle breeze blowing off the water, the office building was filled with chatter and traffic as staff, administration officials, and aides bustled past one another in a perpetual rush hour.

Though I was not an official member of the government, I did come close to at least *looking* the part, having upgraded my dress code to a blazer and tie. At 9:00 a.m., I was led into a small conference room, where a lone pot of coffee greeted me. I took a seat near the head of the long table and waited. And waited. Before long, I grew uncomfortable and anxious as thirty, then forty-five minutes passed. Then, some fifty minutes past our scheduled starting time, the wooden conference room door opened, and in walked the most important man on the planet.

His dark suit was contrasted with a white dress shirt and a royal-blue tie. Attached to his lapel was the familiar Alliance pin with ten white stars against a sky blue background, with a lone gold star in the center. Black Italian leather shoes shone on his feet. I know they were Italian leather as I recognized the brand from a magazine advert on the plane from Brussels to Rome that morning. Flipping through the magazine, I had wondered, *Why are such expensive shoes advertised in a flight magazine? And what kind of person would spend so much money on them?*

I now had my answer.

Jumping to my feet, I greeted the president, and he shook my hand and asked me to sit. He then whispered something to his loyal aide, who nodded compliantly and left the room, shutting the door behind him.

"My deepest apologies for my late arrival. I had to attend to some time-sensitive documents as well as a briefing by my military counsel. Unrest is brewing to the north, and I am not sure we will be able to prevent what is shaping up to be an inevitable conflict." He exhaled slowly. "But I trust some good can come from it. Now, on to our time together. How have you been, De Clercq? It's been a few weeks since we last spoke. I trust you've been given ample access to the source files for your research?"

"Absolutely, Mr. President. Your staff has been most accommodating and helpful to me. The printed documents and the secure online files provided have been very useful and informative."

"Excellent! Now, as for today and tomorrow, I believe we have allotted two one-hour slots for this, so with no time to waste, let's get started, shall we?"

I noticed the president's demeanor was considerably less cordial and relaxed than it had been during our previous interview at the villa. His countenance communicated, "Let's get this done. I'm a busy man." I reminded myself that this appointment with me was only a small part of his agenda, as his itinerary included multiple meetings throughout the day. I glanced down at my prewritten questions.

"Of course, sir." I grabbed my pen while simultaneously hitting Record on my digital device.

"So, Mr. President. Apart from the official background bio provided by your staff and what can easily be ascertained by anyone via an internet search, I wanted to hear more about your background in your own words. The bulk of what I will officially write should come straight from you, sir. This is your story, as told by *you*."

"Right. You said that last time, as I recall," he said, a twinge of impatience in his voice.

"Yes, sir. So, my first question links with our previous conversation regarding your sudden rise to prominence, as previously you were relatively, well, sort of *unknown*. Some have referred to you as 'the Man from Nowhere,' which is an obvious overstatement. But that being said, why don't you take us back to your early, formative years. What made you the man you are today?"

His shoulders relaxed, along with the furrow in his brow that had been lingering since he walked into the room.

"Hmm, formative years," he mused. "Fair enough. And I can appreciate the direction of your inquiry. Stay on track with your questions, and be careful not to try and lead me with them. And don't ever put words into my mouth."

"Absolutely. I won't do that," I responded, feeling a bit rebuked.

"Perhaps I should begin with my dear parents, who, above anyone else, have influenced and marked me. Despite ridiculous internet rumors about my having 'clandestine beginnings,' I came into this world like everyone else. I was born early on the morning of June 6, 1988, at the University of Zurich Hospital, which incidentally traces its beginnings back to the year 1204, making it one of the oldest hospitals in all of Europe. At the time of my birth, my father was enrolled in that university's doctoral program—"

"Pardon the interruption, sir, but may I ask what his field of study was?"

"Good question. He earned his doctorate in banking and finance, soon after which our family returned to Milan, Italy, *his* birth city. As my father rose up the ladder of the banking industry, this precipitated some six moves in twelve years. As a result, I never really developed many, what you might call, 'close friends.' And you may also be surprised to learn I was quite reserved as a child. I kept mostly to myself. From an early age, my mother nurtured me with a great affection for reading. It was a passion we shared. Much of my childhood and adolescent years were spent in libraries, reading nooks, or the rear gardens of our many homes. I would get lost for hours attempting to satiate my voracious appetite for mental stimulation and knowledge, mostly through books on fantasy, history, and philosophy."

"Fantasy, sir? Would you care to expand on that a bit."

He shrugged. "Certainly, though there's not much to say, really. I have long been fascinated with stories of alternate worlds. Civilizations that exist in other times or dimensions. The clashing of battling kingdoms, rival thrones, and realities where supernatural occurrences were commonplace—those kinds of things. As you'll discover, however, my primary passion by far is history . . . and the *real* world."

"Very interesting," I murmured.

Circling back to my original question, he went on.

"Of course, as anyone can learn from my website, my formal education included a bachelor's degree in humanities from the relatively obscure Leiden University in The Hague, Netherlands.

From there, I traveled the short distance to Erasmus University in Rotterdam, where I earned a master's degree in history, specializing in a rather odd combination of ancient history and international relations. But what is missing from that website bio are the two years I spent traveling the world following the completion of my graduate degree."

"Oh? I was unaware that you—"

"Yes, after gorging for years on academia, I became quite anxious to liberate myself from the classroom and study cubicle. So, I packed a bag and traveled to places I had always wanted to visit, sites of particular historical interest to me—America, France, Germany, Russia, Austria, England, Egypt, and Israel. And as I was on no particular timetable, I visited them at leisure, immersing myself as best as I could into those cultures, absorbing knowledge concerning significant events and movements, touring battlefields, studying their governments, and contemplating the impact left behind by their great leaders. I became a constant fixture in numerous museums, spending days upon end poring over historical documents, watching archival footage, and analyzing artifacts and displays of antiquities. Governments. Wars. Rulers. Relics. Weapons. Maps. These were my constant companions."

"Hmm. And did you travel with a friend? Girlfriend?"

"No, no," he laughed. "Mine was a solo adventure all the way. My pace and routine would have been highly incompatible with traveling companions."

"On a side note, sir. You remain undoubtedly one of the world's most eligible bachelors. Is there any particular reason why you have never married? Has there been a significant other? Then or now?"

"Julien, if you're trying to ask me whether I am a homosexual or bisexual, the answer is no. Truth is, I simply don't have a serious desire or interest for a relationship with a woman for one simple reason."

"That being?"

"*Stewardship*," he answered definitively.

"*Stewardship*, sir? I'm afraid I don't follow what you're saying."

"Well, given my daily schedule and perpetually full calendar, I just don't have the luxury to invest the enormous amount of time required for a romantic relationship. I have to be fully committed to my calling. Leadership is my wife and lover. And I must effectively manage my time and gifts in a way that yields the maximum return. I realize that perspective may seem a bit out of place in a day when people are desperate for relationships, but in order to help create a world where others can experience love and family, someone has to make a sacrifice. And that someone is me. So yes, *stewardship*. And besides, trust me: no woman would want to be married to a man like me."

"Got it," I said, making a mental note not to bring up the subject again.

He smiled, twirling a pen on the large oak table. And I returned to the subject at hand, inquiring, "And did you find any one country or experience that stood out to you in those two years of traveling?"

The president paused, as if a conversation were going on in his head, debating whether he should permit himself to divulge further. Then, with a nod of the head, he puckered his lips slightly and continued.

"So, *memorable encounters*. If you will indulge me for a moment, there were three unforgettable experiences which stand out in my mind—London, Jerusalem, Egypt—in that order. I particularly enjoyed my many visits to the British Museum, where I spent a considerable amount of time gazing in wonder at exhibits regarding histories of the most majestic empires on earth, particularly Egypt, Assyria, Babylon, and Rome. All these mighty governments eventually failed or were conquered. My father once remarked to me that during those two years away I likely spent more time with the dead than with the living." He laughed, then acknowledged, "And I suppose he would be right. History, however, can be such a marvelous and seductive mistress, for she always satisfies, while simultaneously imparting wisdom of the ages."

The corners of his mouth turned up. "Oh, and there is also a fascinating antiquarian bookshop just across from the British Museum there in London, sandwiched between shops containing tourist trinkets. You must visit it if you ever go there, Julien. I spent more money than I care to admit in that shop, acquiring first-edition works and military maps from the sixteenth through eighteenth centuries. Often, I dipped into my food budget in order to feed my literary addiction. But missing a few meals is nothing compared to the satisfaction of knowledge gained, right? I was then, and continue to be, a hopeless bibliophile."

An enormous sense of pride beamed from his confession. And yet, there was also a magnetic warmth associated with such arrogance.

"By the way," he added. "I have hundreds of photos from my old travel days. If you think they may be of some use to you in compiling my story, let me know and I will arrange to have them dug up for you."

"Thank you, sir. That might actually be enlightening. I am making note of it."

The president's aide entered suddenly, interrupting our flow of thought. He handed the president a small piece of stationery on which was written something I couldn't read. The president scanned it, then said, "Unacceptable. Tell him my original order stands, and that he best get behind it immediately."

The aide bowed slightly and scurried out of the room.

"Where were we, Julien?"

"Your most memorable experiences?"

"Yes, London. The second experience that comes to mind concerns my time in Jerusalem. This ancient city is a fascinating intersection into which the world's three most prominent religions converge. Each of them makes some claim to this little sliver of the promised land, with Jews and Muslims perpetually at each other's throats over it. Both religions trace their roots to particular sites there, and to a shared patriarch, Abraham. And, of course, the Christians' Jesus was crucified there. But it wasn't primarily the religious significance of the city that intrigued me as much as the measure of human gravity the city represents.

"Specifically, the Temple Mount area aroused my deepest curiosity. As you may know, this portion of the city is sacred in the sense that it has, for centuries, been the focal point for billions of religious seekers. You could argue that this tiny area is sort of a 'Rosetta Stone' for mankind. There, we see both the brilliance as well as the decay of mankind's glory. Through the legends and tales of men like Abraham, Muhammad, and Jesus, we are reminded of the virtues of sacrifice, leadership, and love. And yet the irony is that each of those religions has also brought much conflict, death, and division to the world.

"I only spent two weeks in Jerusalem proper, but while there I imagined what it would be like if the world could someday reimagine this place as a source of human unity instead of division. Sounds just like something an idealistic twenty-five-year-old would say, right? And yet, there remains, I believe, in all of us, a fundamental desire to lay aside our differences and come together in peace and harmony. And I still believe we can do that if we're all properly motivated! So many look to Jerusalem. If she only realized the power of peace that is well within her grasp," he declared, raising his voice a bit. His tone subsided as he snickered, "Now I sound like I am campaigning."

"No, it's fine. Whatever you want to say, sir. There is no script here."

He moved on without acknowledging my comment.

"But two weeks was enough. I spent another few days in

solitude in the surrounding desert. But that's perhaps a story for another time."

I wrote on my pad: "Desert?"

"I suppose my most memorable, and dare I say *mystical*, moments of my world tour came, however, during a visit to the Great Pyramid of Giza. As you may know, it's the most ancient of the seven wonders of the world, and a stunning, intimidating work of design and precision engineering. Rising out of the desert sand at over 450 feet tall and weighing some six million tons, this magnificent structure dwarfs all those who encounter it. And to think, it was built as a tomb for one man—the pharaoh Khufu, from the Fourth Egyptian Dynasty. By the way, if you ever visit the Cairo Museum, you can see a tiny ivory figurine of this pharaoh, whom the Egyptians, of course, hailed as a god. It's just three inches tall, but nevertheless exudes a mysterious power worthy of such a notable ruler."

The president's eyes were fixed in a trancelike gaze as he spoke, as if I were suddenly invisible to him. And then, with a blink, he returned his attention back to me.

"But you were asking about my experience, not a lecture on archaeology. Julien, the real reason I found that particular visit so meaningful was, as I paused to rest on one of those massive granite blocks that formed the pyramid, I was awestruck not only by the structure itself but also by the reason for its existence. Granted, Khufu commissioned the pyramid to be built for himself, but the mere fact that he *could* decree such an undertaking overwhelmed me.

"Contemplating this fact while sitting under a blazing Egyptian sun, it occurred to my young mind how ultimately unique such an accomplishment was. Consider that the vast populace of humankind is made up of billions who do not possess even the slightest portions of purpose or passion. These persons are born . . . and for what? To achieve their maximum potential and make a significant and lasting contribution to mankind? On the contrary. Rather, they go on to lead lives of utter futility, filling their days with work, food, entertainment, and sex. And again, for what?"

The president rose from his chair and strolled to the window overlooking the busy street three stories below. Peering down at the street and sidewalk traffic, he said, "Look at all these people, Julien. What do you think is going through their minds right now? What are they thinking about? Visions of greatness? How to make the world a better place? Thoughts of real significance? No. They're thinking about getting to the next appointment. Where to eat for lunch. What movie they'll watch online later tonight. Worthless mind debris."

His nostrils flared as he turned back to me.

"Mere sheep! They are weak, and are deservedly weeded out by natural process. They become stepping-stones for those who actually know where they're going. And soon they are all forgotten. They join billions whose lives meant nothing. *Less* than nothing. They breathed the air, contaminated the world with their consumerism, all the while taking up valuable space with their presence. So uninspiring. Their days are marked by a meaningless monotony of trivialities, with no thoughts beyond themselves and their immediate urges.

"But just occasionally"—he slowed his cadence, while his enthusiasm remained vibrant—"occasionally, history steps in and saves the day, surprising us—birthing Khufu, Nebuchadnezzar, Alexander the Great, Julius Caesar, or Napoleon. Men like these achieved greatness of a titanic measure, attaining godlike status. They are lifted high, towering over Earth's historical landscape like Himalayan mountain peaks. And that day in Giza, I found myself relaxing against a colossal monument honoring one such individual."

His disgust at the common man had quickly turned pensive. "And while taking a drink from my water bottle," he reflected, "a thought formed in my mind: *Will the world ever witness such majestic greatness again? And if so, what would it look like? And who would achieve it?*

43

"These questions kept reverberating in my brain, so incessantly that I could not dismiss them. And while pondering this human predicament, I heard a voice so clear I would have sworn someone was standing directly behind me. But turning around, I discovered I was all alone, with the exception of a few fellow tourists below at the pyramid's base. The voice I heard simply asked, 'Why not you, Adam?'"

He appeared for a few seconds to be frozen, paralyzed by thought. Then he once again picked up the pen, nervously stroking it with his thumb.

"The experience sent shivers down my back, Julien. I initially attributed the incident to heat exhaustion, as the temperature was blisteringly hot that day. And I also had not yet eaten. I have been exhausted before, even dehydrated. But I've never heard voices inside my head. I have always been one to side with rationality over subjective experiences or silly mysticism. And yet, this incident troubled me the rest of the day and on into the night. Finally, unable to sleep, I arose from my hotel bed and ambled toward the balcony door, thinking a bit of fresh air would do me good. Stepping out onto the terrace, I gazed up into the Egyptian night sky. Ah, the stars shone with such clarity against the velvet heavens that evening. I can still see them. And standing on that terrace, I reflected upon my experience at the pyramid, fondly recalling a proverb often repeated to me by my parents:

> 'One may spend his days learning poetry, history,
>   religion, or science.
> But no greater teacher, and no better friend, is the
>   priceless gift of self-reliance.'

"From childhood, my mother and father taught me this self-reliance as a basic operating principle for survival and success. And as the constellations would guide ancient mariners, since that time I have adopted that principle as my own guiding virtue. Consequently, I have never looked to others for my needs, and never entertained the entitlement mentality that has infected the minds of so many in our day. Instead, I embraced the responsibility and the obligation to look after my own affairs. 'Friends, family, and even lovers will let you down, son,' Father would say, 'but when everyone around you fails, you are inevitably left with yourself. Lean *inward*, son. The answers are found within.'"

"Your parents really did have a profound influence on you, didn't they, sir?"

"Yes. Yes, they did," he sighed. "And I have never forgotten their guidance. Today, I trust no one explicitly but myself. Though some have mistaken this for arrogance or having an air of 'aloofness' about me, nothing could be further from the truth. This autonomous self-government approach is, in reality, a wonderful gift to others and to the world, for it removes the burden for us to unnecessarily depend upon our neighbor. If everyone were responsible to fully care for themselves, the planet would be in a much better place than it is today. The so-called golden rule says to 'do unto others as you would have them do unto you.' But tell me, how can you ever do any good for anyone else if you have first not done good to yourself? You cannot skip over this critical step. It's time we replace the golden rule with the more valuable *Platinum* Rule—'Do unto yourself first, so that you are *able* to do well unto others.'"

"And how would you say this personal philosophy has served you, Mr. President?"

"Perceptive question. To begin with, this self-rule and independence was what saw me through college and graduate school. It's what helped me win my first job in local government among dozens of other well-qualified applicants. It's what drove me to run for election in the Italian Chamber of Deputies, and it enabled my appointment to the Committee on International Relations, which

I eventually chaired. You see, Julien, I had keenly watched from a distance my father's ascent through the ranks of Italy's Unicredit Bank. I don't have to tell you that becoming the chief financial officer of that world-renowned institution didn't happen by accident. His ambition was fueled by a fundamental belief in himself. Without it, he would have been left to the mercy of others and to the changing trends of the banking industry."

I interjected. "So, when the great disappearance last fall occurred—"

"Precisely!" he shot back emphatically, his open palm striking the table.

"This tragic, international crisis created a global leadership vacuum, as countries were virtually imploding by the hour. Simultaneous to this was the infighting and confusion which reigned in their houses of governments. While impotent world leaders wrung their hands in paralyzing confusion and misery, it was then I realized I no longer needed some mystical 'voice from a pyramid' to motivate me. No, it was my *own* voice which spoke to me this time, '*Why not me?*' And, well, here we are. I am occupying what is undeniably the most influential chair on the planet. And it's exactly where I belong. All because of self-reliance."

And with those words came a knock at the conference room door, which then opened. "Mr. President, it's time for your meeting with the Russian ambassador."

The president nodded, turning to me with a self-assured expression. "Antonio," he called out, "what time am I meeting with Julien tomorrow?"

"You're scheduled for 2:00 p.m., sir."

"Right, 2:00 p.m.," he repeated. "Well then, I'll see you tomorrow at two, De Clercq." And he exited the conference room.

"Yes, Mr. President. I look forward to our next interview."

But it was not to be.

CHAPTER FOUR

THE JEWS

What neither the president nor his military intelligence and foreign relations officers knew upon the conclusion of our interview, was that his scheduled meeting with the Russian ambassador was nothing more than a ruse—a cleverly devised deception designed to divert attention from a clandestine troop deployment south toward Israel. Russia was the most prominent nation that had refused to join the Alliance, preferring instead to form its own international coalition of power. That in itself was not inherently problematic. But it was the covert *purpose* of that multinational coalition that proved a threat to world peace. For precisely at noon on the same day, Jerusalem time, the combined armies of Russia, Turkey, Iran, Sudan, Libya, and a handful of additional, smaller nations launched a coordinated military strike against Israel in an attempted invasion of that country.

The administration had been aware of some light troop movement. However, intelligence reports were understated, and the attack achieved complete surprise, especially in the context of the Russian ambassador's assurance *that very day* that rumors of war were unfounded, and that such talk was nothing more than "sword-rattling across borders."

It was later revealed that the president had previously been in negotiations with the Israeli prime minister concerning the signing of an unprecedented peace accord designed to bring stability to that volatile region. Word of these negotiations between the European Alliance and Israel reached the Russian president's ears, who saw it as an opportunity to conceive and form his own alliance. And it wasn't a difficult confederacy to form. The previously mentioned Russian allies were forming their own "United Nations of Islam," and willingly joined the newly created Northern Federation. It is no secret that these Muslim nations have long sought the destruction and eradication of the nation Israel.

Since the vanishing incident some six months earlier, the world's attention had been focused on coming to terms with those missing, and trying to recover from the devastating impact the event had made on civilization. For once, Israel was removed from being the focal point of global tension. And she was relatively unaffected by the event, as were the Muslim nations. The only tangible effect it had was that the United States, formerly Israel's closest and most powerful ally, had been ravaged by this catastrophe, as virtually every segment of America's infrastructure suddenly imploded.

The event severely weakened Washington, DC, crashing Wall Street and crippling her armed forces. America became a country saturated with fear, confusion, and panic, no longer able to come to the aid of Israel because she couldn't even help herself! This was the Platinum Rule the president had told me about, only played out on an international, geopolitical level. The vanishing brought a devastation from which the United States would not recover.

This weakening did not go unnoticed by Russia and its Muslim allies, and they seized the moment, using it to their advantage. But while one might argue that it makes sense to attack Israel while her strongest ally has been rendered impotent, why do it at all? Politicians, pundits, and military experts have all weighed in on this matter. And among the best explanations are that these nations sought control of vast, untapped oil reserves that lay beneath Israeli soil. But oil wasn't their only motivation, as all these countries fundamentally loathe the Jewish people. Before last fall's mass vanishing, anti-Semitism had been on the rise, particularly in European countries. And of course, many of the aforementioned countries have a long history of conflict with Israel, with several Muslim nations calling for the complete eradication of the Jewish race.

We now know that Russian-Muslim ground forces marshaled themselves at Israel's border, essentially surrounding her on all sides. And yet, remarkably, the tiny Jewish nation did nothing. The Israeli Defense Force (IDF), long considered one of the world's best, patiently waited, choosing not to fire the first shot.

This proved to be a strategic move, as Israel avoided the condemnation and criticism of having officially started a war, and thus further fueling the fires of anti-Israeli sentiment worldwide.

But then, something happened that, to this day, continues to puzzle all of us.

Before a single missile was launched, and just after tanks began crossing the northern border into Israel, a great earthquake ripped through the land, derailing the initial attack and killing some 70,000 invading troops! This seismic event also crippled communications between the Russian-led armies, creating mass confusion and causing them to fire on each other by mistake. This was further complicated by the fact that the attacking forces spoke different languages.

The earthquake and subsequent infighting also greatly slowed down medical treatment and transportation of the dead and dying, which further spawned infections and diseases among those injured. And as if that weren't enough, a torrential rain combined with volcanic rocks and ash from a chain of previously dormant volcanoes along the Golan Heights showered down on the attacking military forces. The death toll swelled into the hundreds of thousands, and it all happened without a solitary bullet or rocket fired from the IDF.

But there was a different kind of fallout that resulted from what many now call the "David and Goliath War" (D&G War). It would appear that nature had come to the defense of Israel and the Jewish people. Those living within her borders, however, tell a different story. They claim instead it was their God who fought on their behalf, and that he directly caused this anomalous and peculiar chain of events to occur, thus delivering them from their enemies, much as he supposedly did centuries ago during their exodus from Egypt.

But regardless of how one chooses to explain it, this brief *war* produced four irrefutable results: (1) It garnered a great deal of sympathy for the Jewish people. They were living peacefully and securely in the land before this attempted invasion. And the fact that this attack was unprovoked only added to this global outpouring of sympathy. (2) It effectively wiped out any combined Muslim military force. The majority of Islamic nations had, in effect, "bet it all" on this invasion, and afterward there was not left a viable military infrastructure for any sort of significant ground force or organized terror network. (3) It united the Jewish people, generating a sudden influx of Jewish immigrants into Israel. This "aliyah," or "going up," to Israel effectively emptied the world's nations of their Jewish populations. Virtually all those of the Hebrew race were now calling Israel home. And (4) this proved to be the open door the president was looking for, as his previously proposed peace accord now became both expedient and fitting for the hour. He wisely capitalized on the crisis, seizing the occasion to bring the Israeli prime minister to Rome to sign the agreement.

Among the articles of this agreement, amended and added just one day after the Russia-Muslim invasion debacle, was one awarding the Jews carte blanche access to the Temple Mount area of Jerusalem. This sacred piece of real estate had been partially claimed and occupied by Islam, symbolized by the iconic Al-Aqṣā Mosque compound and the Dome of the Rock, which had stood on the site for more than thirteen hundred years. But all that changed once the Jerusalem Accord was signed. Before the ink had dried, Israeli bulldozers, standing at the ready, razed the Muslim holy site following an initial, brief skirmish with remaining waqf guards, all of whom were killed by IDF soldiers, with Alliance sanction and support. Protests erupted in both Jerusalem and in the Muslim world, but there was no real recourse at their disposal, their countries' militaries having been previously destroyed. Online terrorist bomb threats were made toward both the president and the Israeli prime minister, and arrests were made as security for them was subsequently heightened.

It took just two weeks to clear the rubble from the Mount area, facilitating the rebuilding of the Jewish temple. This was a centuries-long dream come true for the Hebrew people, though blueprints and preparations had been in place since the late 1980s. All that had stood in the way was Islamic control and presence at the site, which has now been removed thanks to the "David and Goliath War," and, of course, the president. This fortuitous series of events further solidified his platform and celebrity status worldwide. For his part, he made sure he profited from the moment, taking full credit for the near-miraculous achievement and peaceful transformation of this formerly unstable region. Even so, Muslims remained infuriated about the whole thing, incited by remaining Islamic imams and a handful of radical terrorist cells scattered throughout the Muslim world.

I sat down with the president to discuss this unexpected victory eight days after the accord was signed and the dust had settled. I found myself back in the same conference room in the Roman office facility, seated in the same chair. And as if scripted, the president was, once again, late, though not quite as overdue as before. He entered the room beaming with an aura of accomplishment, like the proverbial cat that ate the canary.

"De Clercq! Good to see you. Sorry to keep you waiting. Lots going on, as you know!"

"Understandably so, Mr. President. My congratulations on the Jerusalem Accord."

He closed his eyes in a satisfying smirk and nodded. "Yes, it was quite a historic accomplishment. One for the ages, I believe. And who would have thought that such a monumental agreement would initiate out of a near war that could have set the world on fire?"

"Yes, sir. Historians will have plenty of meat to chew on regarding these days, for sure. And yet, you somehow possessed the foresight to get ahead of history by meeting with the Israeli prime minister before any of this occurred. Can you explain that?"

"Well, I suppose some might say it was just great political luck. But as you already know, I don't believe in luck or fate. Believing in yourself is what puts one on the path to success. And I knew that if I reached out to the prime minister, we could potentially work something out between the Jews and the Muslims. I just didn't know we would have help from the most unlikely of sources. Oh, and in case you haven't heard, the Russian government will no longer have an embassy here in Rome, nor will they have one in Babylon when we move there. And that also applies to the Muslim nations who aligned themselves with the Russian president. Those who take peace from the earth do not have a place beside other peace-loving nations. We have effectively sent them out into the wilderness to forage for their own survival, apart from the European Alliance."

Wow, I thought.

The president had been standing since he walked into the room, and only now took a seat at the head of the large wooden conference table. He was brimming with energy, no doubt still buzzing from his historic accomplishment.

"But moving along, De Clercq, were you aware the *Jerusalem Post* this morning called me the 'Man with the Golden Pen,' referring to the monumental significance of my peace accord?"

"I saw that," I replied. "In fact, news sources in every country are praising it as a 'Door to the Dawning of a New Age,' lavishing you with accolades and titles such as"—I glanced down at the notes I had written that morning—"'the Prince Who Brings Peace,' and the *London Times* has referred to your early presidency as 'the New Pax Romana.'"

"Yes, I know. My staff tells me there is already discussion regarding the Nobel Peace Prize. I can't explain how that makes me feel, perhaps a mixture of humility . . . and delight."

I wrote the words *NOBEL PRIZE* in all caps on my pad. It no longer surprised me what this man could accomplish. Was it attributable to his personal philosophy of self-reliance, or was there something else driving his political prosperity? Could it be the team with which he had surrounded himself? Perhaps the mere convergence of events that coincidentally intersected with him at this critical crossroads in time and history? Or was there some other catalyst involved? A force far beyond humanity itself?

Could there be an unseen hand guiding him, and history, forward into a new era? Could any of this be attributed to that "voice" he had heard that day on the pyramid? Or maybe a combination of some, or all, of the above? Personally, I had no idea, and how would I, or anyone else, ever know? All I knew was that this man seemed to combine the charisma, political savvy, personal charm, ambition, leadership, and oratory skills of every great statesman of the last 100 years.

I had originally intended to discuss globalization and the president's vision for how the European Alliance would unite the nations and the world. However, the D&G War and the ensuing Jerusalem Peace Accord preempted that interview, taking top priority.

"Yes, sir. This is world news indeed. If you would allow me to regress for a moment, however, and talk a bit more about the Jews and this unparalleled treaty you so brilliantly brokered with them."

"Ah, the Jews. History's quintessential enigmatic tribe. Julien, I believe that to fully understand the Hebrew people, you have to grasp a sense of humanity itself. Being a student of history like I am affords one the privilege of a wide-angle perspective as opposed to the knee-jerk, myopic views many historical revisionists possess. Put bluntly, the Jews are a peculiar race. They always have been. There has been more written about them and *by* them than perhaps any other people group. That's because to some they represent the ultimate annoyance while to others they are humanity's delightful oddity. But whether they serve as the irritant or the inspiration, the fact remains: you can't ignore them.

"You can't properly survey history and bypass the Jews. They are responsible for two of the world's most prominent religions: Judaism and Christianity. Without Abraham and Jesus Christ, humanity would be vastly different. Of course, Islam claims Abraham as well, as he is the father of both the Jewish and the Arab peoples. At any rate, one trait that perpetually marks the Jews is their uncanny ability to *survive*. While on my postgraduation travels, I came across an evaluation of them in my readings. So impactful was it that I committed the quote to memory. Now, let's see if I can recall it."

He looked up at the ceiling, searching for the file in his mind.

"Ah, yes. I think I've found it," he said, and began to recite:

In hardly any people in the world is the instinct of self-preservation developed more strongly than in the so-called "chosen." Of this, the mere fact of the survival of this race may be considered the best proof. Where is the people which in the last 2,000 years has been exposed to so slight changes of inner disposition, character, etc., as the Jewish people? What people, finally, has gone through greater upheavals than this one—and nevertheless issued from the mightiest catastrophes of mankind unchanged? What an infinitely tough will to live and preserve the species speaks from these facts!

Upon finishing, he looked at me as if I were supposed to be impressed, which, needless to say, I was!

"That's a fascinating citation, sir! And I can't believe you quoted it from memory. I'd like to use it if I may. Can you provide a footnote for me?"

"You don't recognize the reference, De Clercq?"

"No, sir, I am afraid I don't," I apologized.

"Adolf Hitler. *Mein Kampf,* chapter 11, 'Nation and Race.' Cite any edition at your discretion."

"Incredible," I muttered under my breath.

"Ironic, isn't it?" he remarked. "Coming from a man whose regime aggressively pursued the extermination of Jews from Europe. And were it not for the Allied forces—England, Russia, and the United States—he would have succeeded. And beyond this, he would have likely conquered the world, and in the process wiped out the Jews completely. Hmm. It just dawned on me that, due to the events of the last seven months, all three of those countries are no longer considered world powers."

"It does stagger the mind how quickly nations can fall, and new alliances can be established," I responded.

He didn't acknowledge my comment. Instead, he said, "I had

a lot of time to read during my travels. And *Mein Kampf* had definitely been on the menu for some time. Not so much reading these days with my tight schedule, though I do have a book or two on the bedside table. Suffice it to say, I wanted to get into the minds of those who had helped to write history, whether for good or for evil. So, I read a variety of classic works, including the Bible."

"Oh?"

"Yes. You see, Julien. Whether one believes *religiously* in the ancient writings of the Hebrew Bible, there is nevertheless contained within that collection of books a historical record of sorts. Obviously, it's intertwined with legendary tales of miraculous acts done by their god. As the old German expression reminds us, however, you can't 'throw out the baby with the bathwater.'"

"Meaning?" I asked.

"Meaning . . . amid tales of the supernatural, there is embedded a fairly reliable historical record of the Jewish people. We know this because archaeology has borne it out, validating that record. Say what you will about the Hebrews, as odd as they can be compared to the rest of humanity, but one thing you cannot lay at their feet is the fabrication of history. In fact, lying is strictly prohibited in their moral code, particularly among their scribes and priests. Therefore, regarding the chronicle of their existence before the Common Era, what you encounter in the Hebrew Bible is a peculiar people living in a barbaric world.

"And consider this: They were a *separated* group while slaves in Egypt. They wandered *alone* in the desert as nomads. Upon entering their promised land, they were commanded by their leaders to *isolate* themselves from preexisting tribes and nations. And even after their dispersion in the first century, and though scattered to some seventy nations for some two thousand years, they somehow remained distinct, retaining their Jewish heritage. That, by anyone's estimation, is a remarkable accomplishment."

He seems to know a lot about the Jews, I thought. *Or are they just one category among hundreds about which he is well versed?*

"But what history has taught us, I believe, is that when the Jews *are* separate, with their own communities, they do no harm or cause any real disturbance to society. Even so, turmoil, conflict, and persecution seem to always find them, so much so that one might conclude there exists some sort of curse upon them. And yet, they're still here. Look, in recent history, the difference between the Islamic nations and Israel is that the Jews simply wish to survive, while Islam's goal is to rule the world. Thanks to events of late, however, it's unlikely that will ever happen."

He restlessly tapped his fingers on the oak conference table, concluding, "It was fortuitous that the majority of Muslim countries who wanted Israel exterminated were themselves made impotent as a result of this brief skirmish. The Muslim threat to peace was tangible. But now it has been disarmed. End of story."

I saw this as an apropos time to insert a question I had written down.

"And on that topic, sir, the Jews are claiming it was divine intervention from their God that fought and defeated their enemies in this war. How would you respond to such an assertion?"

"Well, I was first confronted with this idea at my luncheon with the Israeli prime minister following the signing of the Jerusalem Accord last week. At the start of our meal, there was a short ceremony where he graciously presented me with an Israeli flag, a signed copy of the classic work *Journey of a People: The Story of Israel* (which I had already read), a written proclamation making me an honorary citizen of Israel, and a clay pot filled with soil excavated from the Temple Mount. He explained that the clay pot represented humanity, while the soil represented the sacredness of the promise their God had made with Abraham regarding the land.

"Then, later on, while we enjoyed an after-dessert coffee, he leaned over to me, whispering, 'The Jewish people are forever grateful to you for your leadership, Mr. President. We will never forget what you have done for us. For this, we are deeply indebted to you. But please understand, respectfully, that it is our God who is responsible for this military victory, and who has secured for us both the land *and* the peace. It is to him we give *all* the glory.'

"The prime minister then slowly leaned back, his eyes still locked with mine in a sober stare, as if attempting to send a message. I met his stare with one of my own, then broke into a smile. 'Mr. Prime Minister, thank you for your kind words of gratitude. Please know that I deeply respect your faith. And I certainly would not dissuade you from your religious beliefs in this important moment for your country. However, let me be equally clear, I think what we can both wholeheartedly celebrate is that the Arab threat has been eliminated, and Israel has retaken the whole Temple Mount. I understand construction on the Jewish temple is already in process, and that fact tells the world that peace and safety have won the day.' And with that, his smile met mine, and we toasted our coffee cups, 'To peace.'"

"Sir, I cannot imagine what that must have felt like."

"No, you can't, Julien. Think about what has just been accomplished. Israel has been the epicenter of global unrest since the mid-twentieth century, the fuse to a volatile powder keg threatening to ignite the planet and plunge us all into war. This is an undeniable fact, regardless of one's personal feelings about the Jews. As you are aware, no secretary of state, ambassador, *or* president has ever brought lasting peace to this unstable area of the world. And much of the conflict had to do with land, specific boundaries and locations to which both Jews and Muslims lay claim. And no location more specific or sacred than the Temple Mount. It is there Muslims claim their prophet Muhammad ascended to heaven. As such, it has been considered a holy site in that religion. For the Jews, however, that thirty-six-acre area has served as the location of their previous temples of worship. And they haven't had a temple in that location since 70 CE. But now they will, all because of me . . . *and a serendipitous aberration of nature.*"

"Mr. President, how do you envision this successful peace agreement helping to move your agenda forward in the coming months and years?"

"Yes, well, it certainly adds to my political résumé, doesn't it? And I believe it positions me to leverage this achievement, allowing us to ascend to new heights of peace and prosperity. My hope is that the ripple effects of this peace will spread to other nations, prompting them to join me."

I agreed, adding, "In fact, in our next session, I would like you to address some of your specific strategies and goals, if you don't mind, sir. And then, at the conclusion of your tenure in office, whenever that may be, we can return to that subject to revisit your thoughts at that time."

"That would be appropriate," he conceded.

"There was just one more question," I said, glancing at my watch, "as I see we only have about two minutes left."

"By all means, ask. That's what we're here for."

"It's just a footnote, really. Not anything of great substance. But apart from the nations under your alliance, you haven't spent much time focusing on other countries, with the exception of Israel, of course. Your overtures of peace toward the Jewish people have caused some to speculate that you may have a bit of a soft spot in your heart for them, and that the reason for this is because you are, in fact, a *Jew.* So, do you possess any Jewish heritage, sir?"

He snickered.

"You're not the first person to ask me that. People assume that because most of the world has been pro-Palestinian and against

Israel that anyone who helps them must himself be a Jew. But to put the rumor to rest, no, my family's rich Italian ancestry extends back hundreds of years. Look at me, Julien. No one could be more Italian. Cut me and I bleed marinara sauce!"

He laughed.

"No, my interest in Israel is purely for the sake of peace. It is simply a means to a greater end, that's all. And as I said, when the Jews are separate and occupied with their own affairs, they are relatively harmless."

Without notes and with only minimal prompting, the president had an amazing command of language, literature, and history. He was able to piece together not only historical events and their contextual significance but also what part they played in civilization's overall story.

"Julien," he said, as if reading my thoughts, "you cannot impact and change history unless you first understand it. The key to the future lies in the past."

The two of us simultaneously looked up at the digital clocks on the wall, displaying time zones across the world. Our time was up. The president smiled as he stood, firmly shaking my hand.

"I hope to see you soon, De Clercq. And if recent events are any indication, it will need to be sooner rather than later, as it appears history has been awakened and we are entering an age of wonders. Besides, I want to make sure my thoughts are freshly recorded as events unfold."

"Absolutely, sir."

Soon after our meeting, while being driven back to my room at the Barocco hotel, I received a text from Nicolas, a former colleague of mine in Brussels.

Did you see this? Thought it might interest you in light of your current job.

Attached was a link to an article written by a Dutch journalist, titled:

Religion Reborn in Year of Global Chaos
Millions Heap Praise on the President's Leadership

Wonder what your new boss thinks of this? What are his personal religious views?? Have you asked him?

That text got me thinking.

CHAPTER
FIVE

OF MANDATES
AND MESSIAHS

O ur train was losing speed, as if beginning its long deceleration
into the Paris station. Looking at my watch, however, I reasoned
this was impossible, as there were yet some forty minutes left in the
journey. As we slowed, passengers looked up from their phones and
began peering out windows to catch a glimpse of what might be
causing this unusual stoppage. Just then we heard the conductor's
voice from the public address system, "Ladies and gentleman, you'll
notice the train is slowing. Be assured, there are no problems with
the train itself or with the railway system. However, it seems there
is an obstruction up ahead on the tracks, and for safety's sake, we've
stopped a few miles short of it to allow our inspection team time
to get to the site and survey the situation. I don't anticipate a long
delay. Thank you for your patience."

A collective groan could be felt reverberating throughout
the passenger cars. I heard patrons complaining in at least three
languages. But with nowhere to go and no real control over the

situation, I reached down to the side satchel at my feet and retrieved my laptop. After opening the password-protected file labeled "P," I scrolled down to the document containing the transcribed notes from my most recent interview. It was both enlightening and revealing.

I will admit, when the president first approached me to take on this important role, I felt a sense of trepidation. Not to mention *intimidation*! I had yet to prove myself as a writer at this level, and privately wondered if I was up to the task. But the more interviews I conducted with him, the more my confidence grew. I attribute much of this to the fact that the president seemed to genuinely trust me.

Roughly six months into his presidency, the administration compound in Babylon was near its completion. Because of this, the president had scheduled to fly there to conduct a final walk-through before the move-in date, graciously inviting me to travel with him on the plane for that trip. It was during this flight that I conducted yet another interview.

Once I boarded the presidential jet, it became immediately clear that this was an aircraft belonging to a head of state. Though not overly large, it was more than adequate, falling somewhere between America's Air Force One and the royal jet of a Saudi king. And it was outfitted with state-of-the-art technology and the most advanced-level communications system. My interview took place in the president's onboard office, only this time we were not alone. Accompanying him was a new face, and one I'd never seen before in his administration. This gentleman's official title was "minister of affairs," a rather catch-all role encompassing everything from press secretary and public relations liaison to chief of staff. In fact, the administration itself was streamlined and small staffed, at least at the senior level. Extensions of each department of state were delegated to the heads of the ten nations who were officially members of the European Alliance.

I would soon learn, however, that this lone individual played a strategic role. He served at the pleasure of the president and was always at his right hand. Whatever needed to be done, the minister of affairs made sure the task was completed. He was, in effect, the implementation arm of the administration, ensuring that strategy became policy that then turned into action.

His nickname among the staff was "the Enforcer," though his security code name was "Preacher." And I could see why. This man had a face for media. His ocean-blue eyes were simultaneously charming and captivating. He had a natural flair for fashion, and it was rumored he owned so many suits he could have opened up his own haberdashery. And his trendy hairstyle matched his modus operandi—nothing out of place or left to chance.

His oratory skills and on-camera presence were second to none, with an uncanny ability to sell whatever talking point or policy the president dictated to him. So, the persuasiveness of a preacher with the enforcing skills of a mob boss had earned him the appropriate nicknames. This was the minister of affairs. Of course, I knew none of this about him that day on board Jet One.

From that moment on, I never saw the president without this man by his side. We were both seated opposite the presidential desk, though the two of us were never formally introduced, which I assumed was a mere oversight. As was my habit, I pressed Record and opened my notebook, and the interview began.

"Mr. President, you have established yourself as the most accomplished diplomat of the twenty-first century. This, no doubt, has only added to your fame and popularity. Now that the European Alliance is intact and fully functioning, what do you see as the over-arching vision of this unique coalition of nations you've assembled?"

The whir of the Rolls-Royce engines blared outside as we began taxiing down the runway. The president reached over, pulling down the window shade, then smiled as he answered.

"It has long been the goal to establish a unified Europe that would rival and even excel the superpower status of the United States. As a partial result of the tragic events of the previous year, that goal has now become a reality. As you may know, there has been a concerted effort to unify European countries going all the way back to the old European Union of six nations in 1957. Your own home country, Belgium, was a part of that union, Julien. The treaty they signed at that time, called the Treaty of Rome, brought together a population of some 220 million people. Sixteen years later, three more countries would join, and in less than thirty years after that original treaty was signed, a new Europe was taking shape, representing some 336 million people. This was an admirable beginning, and we owe a debt of gratitude to those who laid this firm foundation. By the year 2012, there were some twenty-eight countries involved. They came together because of a love of freedom and unity, and because of a joint recognition that the nation-state model could no longer suffice. A new world order was necessary, one where political, economic, and military interests would converge to serve the common good.

"When the catastrophic event of last year occurred, these, along with most nations, entered a geopolitical tailspin. Panic, chaos, and economic implosion was epidemic, requiring many countries to reevaluate their relationship with the global community. Therefore, as a result, a number of them recognized the expediency of joining together with their neighbors to coalesce for mutual benefit. Some of those joint nations sought an even greater, more globally minded union. Italy, my ancestral home, was one of them.

"A hastily formulated World Congress was convened, producing much debate, disagreement, and dissent. But some of those nations found common ground, and out of this came the European Alliance of Nations. Of course, as you know, some of the representative nations are a combination of several countries devastated by the economic black hole created last year. At the time of our formation, several names were put forward to lead this global alliance; however, I was soon recognized as most capable, and duly elected as president by the provisional government of the ten.

"The old United Nations in New York City, as you know, remains in existence, but functions in name only. As such, I believe that organization has become both archaic and ineffective. We no longer need it because the European Alliance is the *true* United Nations. Instead of meeting for the purpose of endless debate and ineffective resolutions, we are actually *one*. And we are leading the world into peace and prosperity."

The minister of affairs, whose name I still did not know, sat to my left, making his own notes. The captain's voice came over the address system, announcing we had just climbed past 10,000 feet.

"Now, you mentioned goals, Julien," the president went on. "Our objectives are simple and achievable. They are: peace, prosperity, safety, and unity. These four pillars are what support this global coalition, enabling us not only to survive but to move forward with hope. And specifically, how will we achieve these objectives, you might ask? The answer is that we will secure peace through strategic agreements and partnerships such as the one I brokered with Israel. Now, at times a measure of force is necessary to achieve and maintain this peace, due to those nations who may oppose harmony and seek to undo our progress. History is replete with those who would seek to divide and deter the international community from living together as one. But we stand ready to meet that challenge and to dissuade them, if necessary, on the battlefield."

The mysterious man to my left nodded in full agreement without lifting his eyes from his handwritten notes.

"But secondly, beyond peace, there is the objective of global *prosperity* for all. For far too long, we have supported an economic model where only certain people are able to thrive. Through my leadership of the European Alliance of Nations, we are crafting a plan whereby every person on the planet would be treated equally. Everyone will possess the ability to buy and sell without hindrance. But in order for that to happen, there must be consensus."

I must have had a confused expression on my face just then, because the president seemed to notice.

"What we mean by this," he said, "is that we all have to be in agreement with the plan. In other words, we must all operate as a global team for the good of the whole. And there can be no room for dissenters or separatists with their own economic agendas."

I still did not grasp his meaning, but I nodded as if I did.

"Safety in this new world is also a top priority of this administration," he continued, "and we will do everything within our power to protect those citizens who come under the umbrella of the European Alliance. We could be facing dark days ahead, with continued threats of war and the challenge of bringing unchecked crime under control. Therefore, the citizens who align themselves with our cause will receive protection provided by our international military and law enforcement units. We will speak more of this in the months to come.

"But just imagine poverty being virtually eradicated. Mothers will no longer have to worry about whether their children will eat. In our plan," he said, cutting his eyes at the man in the chair next to me, "if one of us is suffering, someone else in the system will do his part to contribute toward their need. And the cost per person, when evened out across the globe, is mere pennies, if that. Again, the key that unlocks this financial freedom is the strategy's central principle of connecting us all together as one."

"So, Mr. President, when do you plan to unveil this econom—"

"Soon."

It was obvious that this was all he was willing to divulge at the moment, and I dared not press him for more.

"And finally, unity. From the dawning of time and recorded history, humanity has longed to be one. Peace contributes to this objective, but peace alone cannot accomplish it. Making the world unified is not a decision made by presidents and politicians. Rather, it is a choice that each individual must make. This is where my administration uniquely recognizes the dignity of every human upon the planet. We respect the right of individuals to choose their own destiny. Therefore, each person will be given a choice. I repeat, *no one* will be forced into this plan, but instead will be given the opportunity to select it for himself.

"But let me make one thing abundantly clear. What we will be providing in this program will be personal freedom, economic opportunity, and much-needed hope. And the alternative? Poverty. Desolation. Suffering. And death. This is the world outside the Alliance. Unfortunately, the options given to us these days are neither preferable nor acceptable. Consequently, we must rely on a greater ideal of global solidarity to bring us into the new day."

His words were concise, direct, and definitive, and less cordial than before. And the presence of this third person in the room seemed to bring out an edginess in the president I had not seen to date.

"Eloquently spoken, sir," the man to my left commented.

Finally! I said to myself. *He speaks!* His Caribbean-blue eyes darted upward at his boss, then returned to his notes and, occasionally, his phone.

I followed up with the president, "And what do you say to other world leaders, even your detractors, who have declared they will steadfastly resist your international political platform? In other words, how will you convince countries that have suffered under failed European unions in the past to suddenly capitulate and fall under the umbrella of your proposed coalition of nations?"

"Now, *that* is a very perceptive and pertinent question, Julien.

And a fair one as well. But the answer is simpler than you might think. I will respond to them by, first, asking them to consider my track record. Look at what I have already accomplished in a very short time span. Just a few months ago, we would all agree that our entire planet was in peril. The United States fell under the economic collapse, moral morass, and governmental upheaval that occurred following the loss of so many of its citizens. Mass looting, rioting, an unprecedented uptick of violent crime, and the reordering of its military all took a toll on what once was considered the 'greatest nation on earth.'

"And as you know, this effect was multiplied worldwide in varying degrees, as countries scrambled to make sense of what had happened and the chaotic confusion left behind in its wake. I watched, along with the rest of the world, as governmental leaders panicked, frantically scurrying like rats looking for a way off a sinking ship.

"No one . . . *no one* rose up to propose a rational, internationally viable solution because they were all too busy desperately trying to save themselves. No one called the world together. No one offered problem-solving strategies that would aid every citizen . . . that is, no one but *me*. Imagine what might have happened had we continued down that path of panic. At least for now we've calmed the waters. *I led that.* So, my record speaks for itself. In this dark world, I have appeared as an angel of light.

"Second, I would urge them to realize that isolationism and nationalism are dinosaurs of a bygone era. Fossilized philosophies. They ran their course and had their day. But global unity is the new spirit of patriotism. Through this unfortunate event, where hundreds of millions were lost, we who remain finally have the opportunity to come together . . . as *one people*. No more division or discord. No borders or barriers. We must see this as a new beginning, a second genesis of humanity in which all peoples—great and small—have a seat at the table. We intend to help transnational corporations and countries experience unhindered trade, establishing economic interchange between all peoples.

"Listen: the bottom line is that now we all truly need one another . . . more than ever. We're in this thing together, stuck on this spinning ball in space. So, it is incumbent upon us to make the best of it while we have the opportunity. I would implore the leaders of nations to see this and come on board with us. If not, then they will be left to themselves. The European Alliance is the only lifeboat leaving this sinking ship. And I am the lifeboat captain," the president announced with a swagger.

I furiously scribbled additional thoughts in the margins of my notepad, careful to record, not only his words, but also the passion with which he delivered them.

"What's your next question, Julien?" he asked.

"Yes, sir. In the context of the important issues you have just covered, there has been a recognizable religious resurgence across the world. This is a two-part question, sir. First, what is your personal view of religion itself? And second, how does your administration plan to cooperate or partner with this expression of faith?"

The president leaned back in his chair, swiveling slightly to his right, where his eyes met those of his minister of affairs.

"We were just discussing this very thing earlier today. And we are aware of articles such as the one your friend sent to you. People are talking, and that's good."

I don't remember telling him about that article. In fact, I don't recall mentioning it to anyone.

"I'll begin with some personal thoughts on the matter. Religion has been a part of the human story since primates first evolved and gazed up at the stars and scratched their heads in wonder. Throughout history, we've seen as many religions, philosophies, and superstitions as there are people groups to invent them. It was Karl Marx who famously wrote, 'Religion is the sigh of the oppressed creature, the heart of a heartless world, and the soul of soulless conditions. It is the opium of the people.' I would add, it is also the great placater of the soul. Man created the concept of a supreme being because, quite frankly, it's too painful to admit that we are all alone out here in space. God exists, not in actuality, but by *necessity*. We need him to be there so we can make sense of the world. And so we can blame his nemesis for our problems and the evils *in* the world. And, I suppose, so people can cling to a promise of hope regarding the next life.

"*That's* religion. Granted, an oversimplified explanation, but sufficient nonetheless.

"Having said that, I personally circle back to my own philosophy of self-reliance. Every person expresses his or her self-reliance in their own unique way. Some do it through religion, and I'm okay with that right now. I mean, what does a person's god do for them except give them strength to do what they want and need in life? No matter the source, the end result is the strength that resides in you helps you through life. So, however you think you obtained that strength is irrelevant in light of the fact that you have it in you. Same with peace. Or happiness. Or love. Or whatever value people attribute to their god. Now, there are some religions that are significantly more anti-intellectual than others—such as some of the voodoo religions in Africa or Haiti, or the mystical faiths of the Eastern world.

"When it comes to the big three—Judaism, Christianity, and Islam—you encounter some similarities and also some mutually exclusive claims and differences. For me, Islam is far too barbaric (in its radical forms) and too self-deprecating (in its moderate form) to be preferable. This recent aggression against Israel was final confirmation that Islam will ultimately die a natural death in the new world.

"As it relates to the Judeo-Christian worldview, the god portrayed in those religions seems capricious, unreliable, and frustrating. And why? His commands are erratic and unpredictable. There seems to be no rhyme or reason to why he does what he does. By the same token, prayers are offered to him, but he does not answer. Not only does he turn a deaf ear to his children's cries, but many times he answers with even more pain and calamity. And yet Jews and Christians alike call him a 'good God.' They also say he is a loving God. And a powerful God.

"But if God is loving, he would want to help his children, like any good father. And if God is powerful, he *can* help his children at any time. But Scripture itself tells a different story. He does not always help his children. And not only does he not come to their aid, but he also gives no reason for why he doesn't do so. How can you know if you are ever pleasing this God enough to persuade him to help you with your life?

"The other reason why he is so frustrating is because he supposedly provides all these good things for us to enjoy, but then tells us not to enjoy them. He gives us things to look at, but he tells us not to touch them. He gives us things to touch, but he tells us not to taste them. He creates boundaries like sheep pens and places his children inside them, but then puts wonderful things *outside* the sheep pen and tells the sheep never to wander out there to enjoy them! This seems contradictory to me, and I don't understand it. And this only provokes humanity to do the very things he forbids. The most desirable fruit becomes the forbidden kind."

The president had thought through his argument, and was articulating some things I had felt myself but was unable to express.

"As I've said before, the Hebrew Scriptures are amazingly accurate from an archaeological-historical perspective. The Bible as a whole, however, is not much more than a random collection of fables and fairy tales written by a downtrodden people group in a desperate search for hope and validation.

"That being said, my personal belief is that *man* is the pinnacle of ascension. There is nothing higher, greater, or more glorious than we are. We are the end of the line. The summation of evolution. That therefore makes mankind, in essence, *God*, if you want to call us that. So, if you're going to worship anyone, start with yourself. If you don't serve yourself and take care of yourself, then no one else will. And until such a time comes that a greater entity is revealed to us, logic dictates that we stick to what we know is true and real. And that truth and reality can be found simply by looking in the mirror. Of course, not all humans possess equal intelligence, abilities, and potential, which is even further motivation to better ourselves!"

His answers were impassioned, and it was evident he had spent much time contemplating the subject of religion. The captain's voice broke through on the speaker system, "We have reached our cruising altitude of 32,000 feet."

The brief pause gave the president a chance to relax his demeanor somewhat.

"Julien, I don't mean to insult anyone's faith. On the contrary, I respect each individual's choice to worship as they please, whether fueled by ignorance or by intellect. You can't prevent people from venerating *something*. In fact, *we* believe," he said, looking at his minister of affairs, "the ultimate path to enlightenment is often found through the path of religion. In other words, faith in something greater is like a stop at a train station on a long journey. But it's not your ultimate destination. There is something better, not *up there*"—he pointed to the sky—"but rather *in here*," he concluded, gently touching his chest.

"And how does your administration plan to help facilitate this journey for the masses?" I asked.

The president again swiveled his head to the right. "Pietro, why don't you respond to that, since this falls under your domain."

"Certainly, sir."

So, he does have a name, I thought with a smirk.

The gentleman to my left rose ever so slightly in his chair and turned toward me. His eyes locked with mine. He explained, "In an effort to (a) guide the world into enlightenment, spirituality, and peace; and (b) help channel this new wave of religion into something for the common good, we are implementing a global faith initiative—"

"Global faith initiative?" I repeated.

"Yes," he affirmed. "An ambitious incentive whereby international awareness is created to inspire and comfort during these difficult days. The sudden turn of events of last year created a void, if you will. A cosmic chasm among the collective consciousness of the world's population. As you have been made aware, people the world over are searching for answers, and in the absence of adequate explanations, they desire an alternative. They require a unifying experience made up of divergent, yet converging paths."

"I-I'm sorry," I broke in. "Forgive me, but I'm not following you."

"Then allow me to spare you the philosophical justifications," he replied in a condescending tone. "People of all religions and creeds right now are struggling with doubt and confusion. The day of the segmented, divisive religious extremism is over, and a new era is upon us. We intend to bring together every religious belief system under one tent. Instead of segregated houses of worship, all religions are encouraged to simply 'celebrate the divine' in whatever manner they see fit, as long as it contributes to the common good, the brotherhood of man, and the new world order of the Alliance. This will be a giant leap forward toward the dissolution of our differences and the formation of international human harmony."

"And how will that happen?" I questioned.

The president's minister elaborated. "Beginning tomorrow, I am issuing an executive proclamation from the president designating all places of worship—churches, synagogues, mosques, and temples—as 'Sacred Spaces.' There, no matter what your religious or nonreligious persuasion, you can come and express yourself, worship, sacrifice, pray, pay homage, light a candle or incense . . . whatever your conscience or faith dictates. And because we will all be connected in a global network affiliation, those whose faith was formerly antithetical, or even hostile, to his neighbor can now unite and appreciate the different paths we all take toward the same Divine.

"Having laid the groundwork for this universal enterprise months ago, we have already been assured participation from leadership in virtually every major religion, denomination, sect, faith group, and quasi-religious movement known to man, including non-disturbing elements of the Christian church, non-Orthodox Jews, and Muslims. It also embraces those who practice Eastern mysticism, along with the occult practices, self-motivation gurus, psychic healers, adherents to the earth energy movement, and consciousness consultants. We have seen positive response from those who ascribe to ascending the astral plane though hallucinogenic narcotics, self-love sages, and those within the faith-prosperity industry.

"In a determined effort to be all-inclusive, no recognized group will be excluded, even goddess cults, and those who engage in sexual expression in repurposed temples and churches. Other sacred-space members will be those who aid in the communication of departed spirits, or even ritualistic divination in an effort to make contact with extraterrestrials, who some still think abducted their loved ones. There will be 'channeling churches,' where outside entities can inhabit a person's faculties and speak from the spirit world—if you believe in that sort of thing. We are including telepathy meditation services and trance modems, symposiums concerning the emptying of the mind, even 'meat-free faith,' and 'dieting toward deity.' Transcendental meditation, shamanism, witchcraft, wizardry, sorcery, and tarot readings. There have already been self-proclaimed gurus, Christs, and messiahs gathering followers in the past year. All these will eventually come under one religious roof."

"And what about those who subscribe to no particular religion or faith system, such as atheists or agnostics, like myself?"

"That's not a problem. No one will be forced to be religious. As with the president's economic plan, it's a matter of personal choice."

"You see, Julien," the president broke in. "It's not really about whether any of these faiths or philosophies are true or valid, but rather that the individual is validated. We are going to legitimize every person who joins this international movement. Together, we will 'celebrate the divine' in us all."

"Exactly," Pietro added. "All these channels flow into a collective, world community of the faith, and no doubt some belief systems will lay aside nonessential values and merge together. Our combined energy and spiritual effort will advance the human race, and the world will live as one. At last, the people of Earth will together realize that, all along, every religion possessed portions of the truth, but just not the entirety of it. Like pieces to a puzzle, all religious beliefs have a contribution to make to the complex mosaic of the divine. A traditional understanding of God as an invisible creator is passing. Rather, divinity is more of a human process. And one of discovery and enlightenment. Every person can attain to that godlike consciousness. They must.

"Granted, not everyone will subscribe to this new way of approaching the subject. Some will revert back to archaic belief systems that rely on exclusion and judgment. There are always those who fight against peace and unity. And with the ground breaking for the new Jewish temple, there has been a small resistance among those in Israel, along with a renewed interest in traditional Christianity. But this is merely a patch of 'rough air' on the flight. They'll eventually come around for a smooth landing.

"But since I quietly began this initiative just before the New Year, the vast majority of those from the international community have been overwhelmingly willing to join their brothers and sisters from across the world and heal together. And I believe it has proven the easiest concept to sell because, well, to be frank . . . the time is right. We're becoming one. The Global Faith Initiative, or GFI, and Sacred Spaces—SS—are the new way."

Why have I heard nothing at all about this? I wondered.

The minister clasped his hands together, signaling the end of his spiritual soliloquy. "Wouldn't you agree, Mr. De Clercq, that the time is right?"

"Oh yes!"

I had to admit, it was a well-crafted plan and an effective presentation, albeit extremely ambiguous in places. Religion has traditionally divided people, not unified them. So, I was curious to see how this plan would play out over time. The longer I listened to him, though, the more convinced I became. And this "Pietro" (whose last name I still did not know) was fully persuaded, by both the necessity and efficacy of his Global Faith Initiative, that this strategy would help guide humankind in its collective quest to wrestle some meaning out of all this madness.

Parenthetically, I felt like he complemented the president well. The two of them shared a similar style, though I couldn't quite put my finger on why. All I knew was, whatever he was selling, I was buying.

Just then, we felt the jet engines throttle back, indicating our initial descent into Babylon. The president spoke, wrapping up the session. "As my chief advisor, Pietro will act on my behalf with the full authority of the office of the president. He is my official mouthpiece and implementation arm. He speaks for me."

As we made our final approach, I wondered why the president had chosen this remote location as his world headquarters. I would soon learn that this region of the world is home to some two-thirds of the world's richest oil reserves. It also sat in a strategic geographic location, at the intersection of several key nations. Once again, the president demonstrated an almost prophetic political acumen. For him, Babylon was also an ancient symbol, a historically powerful city that was once again rising out of the desert sand to claim its prominence in the world.

Jet One touched down, and I found myself on a runway that a year ago didn't even exist.

CHAPTER SIX

"I AM THAT MAN"

As it turns out, a small riot had broken out in the relatively obscure French town of Roye, spilling over onto the rail tracks, causing the obstruction. Protests such as these had become quite common of late, as jobless citizens demanded increasing aid from local and national governments. A semitruck had to be moved off the tracks, and soon we were on our way again. But the longer we had been delayed, the higher my anxiety level had risen.

In a highly mobile world such as ours, travel is one of those luxurious necessities we often take for granted. We instantly communicate, whether by voice, text, or video chat, with someone from across the world. This is a reality those in my generation have always known. But we also take for granted other things as well—like our health. Or that the sun will faithfully show up every morning, and that the constant and calm sky above will always be there to greet us.

Sadly, these expected things are not guaranteed, are they? And when one is deprived of said comforts, we feel a tangible and personal loss. Even more so, when such things are taken from us on a global scale, the mass of humanity, and even the earth itself, groans and suffers.

And yet, that's precisely what happened a little over three years ago.

. . .

Having arrived at the Babylon headquarters, the president, his minister of affairs, and I toured the newly completed office complex, which had been built adjacent to the ruins of the old city of Babylon. This sprawling compound was erected to house the main offices of the European Alliance administration, including an additional ten offices for the representative heads of state, though they were not permanently on-site.

The complex also included the administration's executive staff, the economic advisory team, the office of the minister of affairs (the largest office with the exception of the presidential wing), the military high counsel, and the president's personal security detail. There were also adjacent buildings containing the offices of other support staff and sublevel government agents and personnel. These facilities were diminutive compared to those in most sovereign nations. But special attention had been given and effort made to trim the administration's size to avoid unnecessary bureaucracy and to ensure maximum efficiency. The ten coalition nations composing the strategic alliance all maintained and managed their own branches of the government from their respective countries.

Curiously absent from the Babylonian complex, however, was a space provided for an international press corp. It had been decided early on in his administration that press conferences would be handled digitally, and that all official press releases would be handled through the minister of affair's office and disseminated to the world's news agencies accordingly. This fact highlighted even more the fortuitous opportunity that had been given to me at the president's inaugural press conference.

Construction on this governmental office facility was complete, thanks to crews working in around-the-clock shifts for nearly a year. Though not officially acknowledged, no doubt there were hidden underground bunkers, pre-dug below the main building for the president's protection in the unlikely event of an attack. This way, the survival and function of the government would continue.

Archaeological digs in Babylon, along with the ongoing rebuilding of the ancient city itself, continued as well during this period. Historical tours would carry on as always, and be expanded with new discoveries and continued construction. One interesting footnote is in order here. From the moment of our arrival there, the president's minister of affairs (Pietro) wore a sly smile on his face, as if he knew something the rest of us didn't. And as it turns out, he did.

On our short walk to the administration's main building, we passed the entrance to the old city of Babylon. That's when I heard the president audibly gasp. And the reason soon became obvious. For there, right before us, was an ominous facade leading into the old city proper. I learned that this was the original Ishtar Gate of ancient Babylon, which had been removed from this very site back in 1899 by a German archaeologist named Robert Koldewey. Koldewey and his team painstakingly moved thousands of the glazed blue bricks, later reconstructing them in the Pergamon Museum of Berlin. And there it has remained from 1930 until now, some 100 years later.

Other, smaller portions of the gate were scattered among a handful of museums across the world. They had all been located and procured. Carefully and covertly disassembled by a team of archaeological specialists, this ancient structure, which was previously known as one of the seven wonders of the ancient world, was relocated and rebuilt in Babylon just in time for the president's visit. Originally built during the reign of Nebuchadnezzar II, the Ishtar Gate was named after their goddess of love, war, and sex. There, on the glossy tiles, were varying rows of reliefs depicting bulls, lions, and a dragon-like creature with a snake's head, menacing horns, and a long, forked tongue that spewed fire. The grand entranceway signified that "Ishtar repels her enemies."

While the three of us stood admiring the glorious gateway, I then realized why the minister of affairs had been smiling. This was his personal "welcome home" gift to the president, made possible by Pietro's own executive order and ultimatum to the fledgling German government to release it. The look on his boss's face was all the minister needed to know this present was well received and appreciated.

After inspecting the office facilities, we came to another impressive structure, this one a colossal palace, which would serve as the president's personal residence. This palace had been abandoned by former Iraqi dictator Saddam Hussein when his regime was toppled in the dawning hours of the twenty-first century. It, too, had been hastily updated for the president. A state-of-the-art telecommunications center was installed, along with extensive security and surveillance systems. It also housed a small medical facility. Removed was graffiti left by American and Polish troops when Saddam's regime fell.

"Saddam Hussein had no idea at the time that he was building this for me," the president quipped as we strolled through the palatial rooms and halls.

But unfortunately, our stay in Babylon was unexpectedly cut short by troubling news from the West. Threatening rhetoric and simmering conflict between non-Alliance countries had escalated to the point of an intercontinental ballistic missile launch. This military action provoked additional retaliatory strikes, culminating in the unthinkable.

A nuclear detonation.

At the time, intelligence reports indicated that a dozen or so countries were in possession of such a deployable weapon. And about a third of those nations ultimately chose to exercise that disastrous option. Preexisting peace treaties and weapons reduction agreements between nations were ignored and made void. In a day, four cities in North America were decimated, along with three national capitals in eastern Europe.

This was precisely the scenario the president and his team had feared the most, especially in light of the fact that he had lobbied himself into power riding a platform of peace and safety. Now both seemed to be disintegrating before his eyes.

Mankind had once again managed to turn tranquility into turmoil, erupting into yet another world war. There had been rumors of wars for years before this, particularly after last year's vanishing and its crippling effects on geopolitics in the international community. But despite the president's (and the Alliance's) calls for peace, negotiation, and further invitations to join the coalition, independent-minded world leaders and rogue government regimes refused to sit at the table for talks. Tensions built as stronger nations sought to dominate and conquer weaker ones. It was all about power. And harvesting resources. It was during this time that one northern European leader uttered his now-famous threat, "We will do our 'peace talking' through the mouths of gun barrels, and sign our treaties with the blood of our enemies." His words proved to be a foreboding prophecy.

Such action by these uncooperative nations was a direct threat to the peace the president had so ably established. The sudden, cataclysmic war forced him to respond in kind, deploying coalition armies to face off with those countries that had acted as aggressors.

And his reaction upon hearing the news regarding the first strike? Anger. No, make that *rage*. I know because I saw it with my own eyes. I had never witnessed his demeanor be so furious. Word came to him while he was enjoying a tour of his newly renovated presidential residence in Babylon. And upon hearing it, he immediately called an emergency meeting of his administration's chief advisors and military leaders back in Rome.

The three of us were rushed from the residence and driven back to the presidential jet, whereupon we would soon swiftly take off for the return flight to Rome. In the hurried drive from the palace to the airport, however, I overheard him order someone on the phone to launch a retaliatory air strike as a quick response of retribution, as well as to prepare for a ground forces campaign. He also commanded an expedited movement of the administration headquarters from Rome to Babylon to commence at once.

"Do it now!" he emphatically directed.

Within a week, the move was completed.

Meanwhile, the initial death toll from the multiple nuclear detonations was reportedly well into the millions. But by the time Jet One became airborne, that number had exponentially increased. More battles and devastation would follow, though fortunately none employed the nuclear option. As far as human losses were concerned, those bodies not instantly incinerated by the blasts were burned and mangled beyond recognition. Many would never be found. This would make an official accounting of the dead nearly impossible. Several metropolitan cities were rendered uninhabitable. The soil of nations became saturated with blood, the air pregnant with smoke, ash, and the putrid decay of death.

I still find it difficult to believe. It's an international nightmare horrifically come to life. But sadly, the vaporizing of cities proved to be only the beginning of this surreal reality, as the war effectively sent a number of countries into full-scale economic collapse. The resulting financial sinkhole was so broad, deep, and catastrophic that multiple countries' currencies lost their buying power altogether. Many had barely maintained solvency following the previous year's events, but now there was nothing to rescue them from the economic abyss of total bankruptcy.

Not surprisingly, runaway inflation soared to unprecedented, epidemic proportions. Overnight, citizens who had survived the wars were suddenly transformed into starving, homeless refugees. And yet, the wealthy still managed to weather the storm, insulated, at least financially, from this abominable disaster.

In the days that followed, we began seeing the harmful effects from radioactive fallout. The lingering particle poison was unavoidable. Not only was it airborne, traveling high into the atmosphere and dispersed worldwide, but it also contaminated the soil because of the groundburst effect. Space does not permit me to adequately describe the onslaught of victims inundating hospitals and temporary military medical facilities in the affected areas. Vomiting. Hair loss. Pulmonary edema. Multiple forms of cancer and infectious diseases—all tragically resulted from these detonations, affecting untold millions.

Following this came *more* fallout, but of a different sort. Widespread famine, historically confined to third world countries, found its way into the metropolitan areas of developed democracies, commonwealths, and kingdoms. Even those in the middle class were deprived of sufficient food, and there was nothing that could be done about it. Contaminated vegetables and other food products remained untouched and uneaten as they rotted on market shelves. Radiation exposure remains a formidable enemy, threatening us on many fronts. In areas generally unaffected by the wars, hysteria ensued as panic-stricken consumers swiftly bought up edible resources. There simply wasn't an adequate supply of food, nor a sufficient and expeditious manner by which to transport or distribute what actually was available.

Transportation industries and distribution centers were paralyzed, completely shut down due to war. Not that it really mattered, as subsequent inflation due to high demand and low supplies made even staple foods unattainable. In some locations, an entire day's work was hardly enough to purchase a loaf of bread. Many were driven to eating animal food . . . when it could be found. Emergency services were scarce, intermittently accessible to those in need. Thousands perished while waiting for food and medical attention.

War and famine were certainly devastating enough. No one would argue this. But following these calamities came a rather unexpected and unparalleled consequence—the outbreak of disease brought on by breeding colonies of *rats*. Inhabiting mostly sewers, basements, and the interiors of houses and buildings, these hideous beasts somehow managed to survive the initial nuclear blasts, afterward emerging to feed on the decaying corpses.

The rabid rodents soon became emboldened, claiming territories as it were, attacking, biting, and infecting humans as they ran wild in the streets. These vile vermin overtook homes where families had once lived. And it seemed there was no getting rid of them as the infestation continued to spread. Other animals, such as birds, dogs, and farm animals, spawned additional strains of infectious diseases, contributing to even further food shortages. The contagion epidemic, a deadly aftereffect of nuclear war, made history's bubonic plague seem like a common cold by comparison.

This unimaginable scenario also led to further chaos, crime, and theft. Murder, too, as people desperately sought answers, looking for any reason to explain this evil pestilence, and any people group they might blame for their suffering. And eventually, they found one.

Fear morphed into irrationality, which turned to vengeful rage. Isolated pockets of newly converted Christian believers were identified and targeted, becoming scapegoats and objects of hate. And why? Because they allegedly heralded a message of judgment, claiming these recent world wars and woes were a direct consequence of divine retribution from their God upon humanity for its rebellion against him. Thousands of Christian lives were taken wherever they were found, either by independent law enforcement or by incensed, starving, vindictive citizens. These murders were barbaric in nature, and reminiscent of Middle Ages brutality. Apart from shootings, other executions such as stabbings, stonings, and even beheadings were commonplace. The religion whose savior had died by shedding his blood now saw his devotees' blood being spilt.

The most accurate estimates from the wars eventually placed the total number of dead and missing at close to 1.5 *billion*. But who can know with certainty? Ours became a world seized by a new strain of terror, evidenced not only by charred, bloodied, diseased corpses but also by the psychological effect this war and its aftermath had on the rest of us survivors. A mania was spawned, a *madness*, if you will. Having already lost its sense of peace and civility, the world now abandoned rationality as well.

But sadly, there were even more cosmic disturbances to come.

Not long after this, massive, cross-continental earthquakes provoked numerous volcanic eruptions, spewing unbelievable amounts of toxic ash upward into the atmosphere. Carried by prevailing winds, this thick, volcanic powder all but snuffed out the sun's rays, reducing our planet's source of light to a circular, charcoal silhouette. This atmospheric aberration proved to be a near-universal breaking point as multitudes fled their ash-filled homes, seeking shelter in mountains and caves, like primitive man. It was as if a giant hand had gripped us all with terror, affecting the great and the small, rich and poor. Suicide attempts greatly escalated during those days. And again, many popularly blamed the Judeo-Christian God for it all, though ironically this season of suffering also stoked the fires of religion that had begun when millions vanished the previous year.

Amazingly, the president, though initially enraged, was resolute and determined to stabilize the situation, vowing to capitalize on it and restore peace and stability worldwide.

When we arrived at the Babylon airfield, Jet One was waiting on the tarmac, her engines idling and ready for takeoff. I remember feeling a twinge of anxiety upon exiting the car, turning my walk into a jog as I ascended the stairs leading on board. I did not see the president once during the return flight to Rome, as he and Pietro retreated behind closed doors, presumably to discuss plans on how to deal with this international crisis.

How would he respond from a military and humanitarian perspective? What could be done to steady a shaken populace and restore any sense of hope? How many more would die waiting for aid? Could he manage to keep widespread panic at bay? How would he reach out to countries who had, by their own stubborn choice, left themselves unprotected by the Alliance?

All these questions swirled around in my head as I sat alone in an unoccupied section of the plane, nervously nursing a bottle of water and attempting to faithfully transcribe a written account of the day's events. It is said that great leaders are born in hours of crisis, and I waited with expectation to see how the poised and capable man in the room down the hall would emerge from the smoke of this global emergency. As it turns out, I didn't have to wait too long for my answer.

After touching down at the da Vinci airport, Jet One slowly taxied to a stop outside the designated private terminal. The president, his political companion, and their security entourage deplaned and were immediately whisked away in a black sedan. I collected my satchel and made my way to the forward door. Upon exiting, I was struck with how peaceful it seemed outside. While confusion and hysteria were filling the streets elsewhere, the president's world remained protected, like the eye of a storm. As I prepared to descend the airstairs, I was approached by a female steward who, without a word, handed me a folded piece of paper. Glancing down, I saw on one side of the paper (which proved to be a napkin) the presidential seal of the European Alliance. Once at the bottom of the stairs, I unfolded it. The message read:

Julien,

As I recall, it was your native country's former prime minister who, while calling for international cooperation between nations, famously said in 1957, "We need no commission, we have already too many. What we need is a man who is great enough to be able to keep all the people in subjection to himself and to lift us out of the economic bog into which we threaten to sink. Send us such a man. Be he a god or a devil, we will accept him."

I AM that man.

See you soon,

A.

THE SWORD

I remember thinking it would take decades to recover from this awful war and its residual effects. And I was not alone in my assessment. One look at photos and news footage from the decimated areas was enough for anyone to see that some areas would never be the same again. Aside from the staggering death toll, rampant disease, and economic implosions was the colossal task of how to rebuild the affected cities, if this was even a feasible objective. It took more than two months to extinguish leftover smoldering fires.

Reports from the World Health Organization (WHO) and the American-based RadNet, which monitors levels of radiation in the air, rain, and drinking water, estimated that, due to continued infection and radiation contamination, it would be years before those hardest-hit areas would be habitable. This revelation not only displaced millions more but effectively sent a new wave of "citizen immigrants" flooding into their own countries' urban areas in search of food, shelter, housing, and employment. And this influx doesn't even take into account the number of hospitals perpetually filled beyond capacity with those in dire need of medical treatment.

Designated quarantine units were hastily created to isolate patients with infectious diseases.

And despite the declaration of martial law in several nations, rampant, unchecked crime continued among the displaced and desperate. Prison populations also quadrupled in the months that followed, necessitating the creation of additional incarceration camps because there was simply no available space in already over-crowded jails and penitentiaries. Escapes were not uncommon.

The Alliance army, navy, and air force assisted where they could, providing both humanitarian aid and support to those law enforcement agencies and militaries whose basic infrastructure remained intact following the wars. This included the flying and ferrying of food and medical supplies to ports, which were then transported by military trucks to assigned distribution areas. Some shipments were hijacked by pirates and roving bands of thieves. Nothing was safe or sacred anymore.

Life managed to carry on, however, and within two years, despite ongoing issues related to the war, news connected to it eventually moved from the headlines. And apart from occasional follow-up reports, it hardly appeared in most online news feeds. I think we just wanted to move on to a better place, and not to dwell on the negativity of the past. Our way of coping was to designate a yearly Remembrance Day, where countries everywhere paused at noon for a moment of silence to honor those who had lost their lives in this short-lived war. And so, practically speaking, unless you lived near one of the affected regions or knew someone personally impacted, it was somewhat suppressed in our collective conscious-ness, almost disappearing from our mental radar.

"The dust will settle, and *together* we will overcome this tragedy," the president had declared in a world broadcast just days after the nuclear hostility ended. Because of its timelessness and gravity, his complete address follows:

Citizens of the world, and peace-loving persons everywhere:

Nuclear war. A dreaded, dark phrase the world had never heard until it was coined nearly a century ago. At that time, it was hoped that the mere mention of those two words would deter the potential total annihilation of our species. Those words were meant to serve as an alarm, to awake us, and to strike a chord of terror within the human heart. And they did. They were intended to remind us that we continue to exist here only by virtue of a unifying choice we make—the choice to live in peace, in spite of disagreements and tensions between us. We have already seen, in the past year, efforts to take peace from us in the vicious, multinational attack on the tiny Jewish nation of Israel. Fortunately, that particular micro-war did not have the opportunity to escalate into a nuclear option, as nature fortuitously intervened on Israel's behalf. And though many lives were lost, a peaceful outcome resulted, and a longtime threat from terrorist nations was finally extinguished.

You will recall in the previous year, when well over 100 million vanished without a trace, panic and chaos swept the globe, and many doomsdayers heralded this happening to be a harbinger of the end. But as you know, the end did not come, did it? And in spite of the fragility and volatility of the previous twelve months, I, along with many others in the international community, still believed we could all retain a corporate sense of dignity and restraint. Sadly, we were wrong. But notwithstanding the awful events of this past week, I am firmly convinced we can move forward with confidence and optimism. Therefore, I would like to submit to you three poignant thoughts I trust will serve to dissuade our grief, replacing it with a vision of assured hope for the future. They are as follows:

First, from this moment on, I am calling for the manufacture and deployment of nuclear weapons to be wholeheartedly condemned by every president, prime minister, king, queen, dictator, chairman, and head of state worldwide. We must, I repeat, *must* achieve both unity and unanimity regarding this issue. There can be no dissenters, and no exceptions to this mutually consensual agreement.

Second, we learned an invaluable lesson through this grim situation—that we *can* survive such crises when we are self-reliant and determined. Look around. Despite a horrendous death count and the havoc and devastation this brief war brought, the world nevertheless did not cease spinning simply because a few countries refused to work out their differences at the peace table. As we look back and reflect on history, we observe how our predecessors on this planet remarkably endured, not one, but *two* world wars, as well as other regional conflicts and ongoing campaigns of the twentieth century.

But following each of these, what did we do? We came together. We rebuilt cities and even nations, and eventually became better global neighbors to one another. It goes without saying that my administration will continue working with ongoing efforts to rebuild the infrastructure of cities and communities where possible. And as I speak, we are also reaching out to form strategic partnerships with other like-minded, compassionate nations, offering emergency medical treatment for the victims of this war. We are prioritizing those who have been gravely wounded, as well as children. And we will offer this aid at no cost to them. This is my pledge to you. The dust will settle, and *together*, we will overcome this adversity.

Third, I ask you, "Who emerged as the victor in this war?" The answer? *No one.* The strong sought to conquer the weak and to ignore my coalition's offer of inclusion. But, no. There are no winners here, nor *can* there be in such a conflict. This undeniable fact only highlights the futility of employing the nuclear option. It should convince us of the uselessness of war in this new age of peace. Therefore, tonight, I am hereby proposing a new global peace initiative to the nations. As of this moment, via executive order, I declare that all European Alliance nations will begin immediately dismantling their nuclear weapons cache *on the condition* that every other nation *verifiably* do the same.

Only this course of action can stem the terrible tide of a war such as we have just witnessed and endured. This plan alone can guarantee the protection of nations and the perpetuity of peace. I offer this new policy as an olive branch from the tree of universal peace. It will serve to guide us into a new day and ensure that this generation and the next will be marked by reconciliation and amity, not hostility and death. It is imperative that we look beyond that which divides us or makes us different. Instead, we should see one another as friends—better, *brothers and sisters* united in a global family. Tonight, a preliminary draft of this peace initiative is being delivered to the leadership of every functioning government across the world. A final version will follow within days. It will be simple, direct, clear, and most importantly, *conciliatory*.

Leaders of the world, I await your response. You have seven days.

And finally, to all who fall under the sound of my voice, may a new world conscience now light the way, leading us to a new horizon of peace, prosperity, and safety for all. Good night.

The response to the president's speech was precisely as he and his team had anticipated. The general populace worldwide overwhelmingly responded with enthusiasm and support. The morning after his address, poll numbers showed his popularity soaring to 92 percent, his highest since taking office. Among the leadership of nations, however, there was a mixed reaction, with about 65 percent verbally praising him, 30 percent calling the speech unrealistic, and 5 percent with no noticeable response whatsoever. Over the next six months, a growing number of countries signed on to his Global Peace Proposal. Granted, the vast majority of those consenting countries had no preexisting nuclear program. Even so, it was in their best interests to sign the initiative, as they had nothing to lose and everything to gain.

Concerning the dozen or so nations who were nuclear-ready, all but three embraced the agreement. This triune refusal to comply prompted two immediate responses from the president. First, he assembled a nonpartisan federation called the International Committee for Nonproliferation and Disarmament (ICND), made up of scientists and diplomatic representatives from all countries who had signed the Global Peace Proposal (GPP). They were tasked with regularly visiting every existing nuclear facility and storage site to monitor the deactivation of weapons and dismantling of stockpiles. Further, their duties also involve randomly testing sites for the purpose of verifying that each country remains in compliance with the terms of the GPP.

Second, the president led efforts to apply strict sanctions against those three countries who refused to sign the proposal. These restrictions included trade sanctions, penalties, and embargos, in addition to nonrecognition as members of the global community. Put simply, the three nations were essentially "decapitated" from the global commercial body of trade. This, in essence, forced them into only being able to trade with one another. The net result was that this punitive action cut deeply into their citizens' ability to purchase goods and food products previously available in abundance, whether imported or online. In addition, any transport from these three nations found to be trafficking in international waters risked the seizure of the vessel and confiscation of its cargo. These harsh measures were put into place in hopes of pressuring the three into acquiescing and complying with the demands of the president's Global Peace Proposal.

They never did.

In spite of the president's rigid, unyielding approach here, my repeated exposure to him in our interview sessions convinced me that he didn't find it beneficial to dwell on such negativity, but rather to always point forward and toward positivity. Learning from the past was encouraged, but *dwelling* on the past was prohibited. He was a driven man, yet cordial in his dealings. When threatened or resisted, however, his demeanor could abruptly change, becoming indignant and ironhanded. I witnessed this firsthand through several instances of reprimands and brutal firings within his own administration. So, if a lack of flexibility occasionally marked his working relationship with those closest to him, foreign nations would more quickly feel the wrath of his impatience and unwavering pursuit of his objectives.

"Get on the train, or get on the *track*," I once heard him remark in a phone conversation. Ultimately, you joined his agenda, or you suffered the consequences of not doing so.

· · ·

I felt rather emotionless, perhaps still shocked by the news of the president's death as the Thalys train began its deceleration and approached platform 18 of Paris's Nord station. What had in the past been a comparatively quick commute had turned into a prolonged excursion due to the unexpected delay on the tracks. Before coming to a complete stop, I grabbed my overnight bag and satchel and headed for the train car's external door. Internet service had been uncharacteristically spotty on the trip, and only returned as we pulled in to the station. Having already booked my airport taxi before boarding the train, I had only to locate the driver at the designated pickup spot and then make the forty-minute ride to Charles de Gaulle Airport. Even so, I was concerned that my late arrival would cause problems, but it was not so. I still had a sufficient window of time to make my flight.

A native Parisian, my cab driver was cordial and informative, but frantic and erratic in his driving. I surmised this was due to the president's death, about which he droned on and on (in French). Fortunately for me, French is the second most-spoken language in Belgium, and as a result, I am fluent. *Unfortunately* for him, however, I wasn't in the mood for forty minutes of conversation regarding my boss's violent and untimely passing. With phone service now fully functional, a myriad of messages and emails began flooding my screen.

"Sorry. If you don't mind, I need to catch up on some correspondences," I politely explained to my driver.

"*Je m'excuse,*" he apologized. "*Bien sûr, monsieur.*"

The first text I received was from Marc, a close friend and former university classmate.

Hey, have you seen this? What do we know? Is this reliable?

Attached was a link to a news report from Euro-Now, one of the big three news agencies in western Europe. What Marc didn't know was that I actually knew less than he did regarding the matter. Indeed, I knew less than *anyone*, as further specifics concerning the president's sudden death had been all but nonexistent for those of us on the train. But what I did know from history and experience was that anytime a shocking event such as this occurs, the first casualty is typically the truth, as rumors, hearsay, and sensational headlines tend to overshadow actual reliable details. I guessed this event would be no different. And after clicking on the link, my suspicions were confirmed. The *Euro-Now* article read:

ALLIANCE PRESIDENT SLAIN!

- Assassin Immediately Gunned Down
- Alliance Administration in Panic Mode
- Future of Peace in Peril
- Minister of Affairs Takes Charge
- Was There a Conspiracy?
- Details of the Assassination: What We Know

Placed beside these spectacular headlines were two media boxes, one containing a video and the other a photo of a blood-stained concrete area. I reached into my satchel and retrieved my earphones, put them in, and clicked on the first box. It was an amateur phone video showing a man rushing past a crowd, presumably toward the president, and shouting something un-intelligible. Simultaneously, an indiscernible sound is heard, and then more shouts, accompanied by a chorus of screams. At this point, the camera is jarred, blurring its view, after which it is knocked to the ground, where it lands lens down. All this happens in roughly five seconds.

While the screen remains dark, the audio nevertheless reveals what appears to be a massive shuffle among the crowd, and then the phone is apparently kicked. The sound of rapid gunfire reverberates, eliciting still more screaming and shouting. Someone, presumably from the presidential security detail, can be heard yelling, "Medical! Medical! One is down! I repeat, One. Is. Down!" Other voices can also be detected. "Back away! Move!" "Suspect neutralized! Where the hell is medical!"

Sirens blare in the distance, then become much louder. Within seconds, the screeching of tires is heard. "Inside! Get him inside! Go! Go!" A door slams and a vehicle takes off. "No one leaves this area!" another voice calls out.

All this is audio only. But then the phone is suddenly picked up, and just for a few seconds, a woman's face is detectable, though only from the nose down. She appears to be of Middle Eastern descent, wearing a hijab, and tears are staining her cheeks. Her hands, and therefore the phone, are shaking.

"Ma'am, I need that phone," a man's voice says. The woman questions the man and his authority, and after what sounds like a brief scuffle, the woman escapes into the crowd as the man continues calling out after her. Then the video abruptly stops. She apparently escaped and contacted a media outlet, since the video's dramatic footage eventually found its way onto *Euro-Now*.

The drama and intensity of the audio alone deeply disturbed me, even though the recording yielded very little definitive or reliable information. I looked up to catch the driver's eyes staring at me in the rearview mirror.

"Just get me to de Gaulle, okay?" I snapped.

Scrolling down through the other links, I clicked on "Details of the Assassination: What We Know."

The copy read:

Babylon—

Status: CONFIRMED. At approximately 9 p.m., Arabian Standard Time, the president of the European Alliance was brutally attacked and killed by a lone assassin. The knife-wielding attacker broke through a cordoned area outside a restaurant just a few blocks from the administration's office compound. Reportedly shouting "Allahu Akbar!"

the alleged assailant brandished a machete-sized sword, striking the president, sources say, just above the left ear. The man was then promptly rushed and gunned down by a spray of bullets from security agents, while immediate attention was given to the fallen leader. A frantic effort was made at the scene to contain the bleeding from the massive head wound. Within seconds, a motorcade sedan arrived, and the president's lifeless body was hurriedly placed inside. The vehicle sped off to the medical wing of the palace, where a team of emergency physicians stood at the ready, awaiting his arrival. Once inside, doctors and trauma surgeons labored furiously in an attempt to arrest the blood loss from the gaping wound. However, after 30 minutes of administering continual lifesaving procedures, it became clear to all present that there was no life left in the world's most prominent political leader. The president was officially pronounced dead at 9:41 p.m.

In a hastily arranged press conference in the palace foyer, the president's surgeon, Dr. Paolo Giodarno, made the following remarks in a video broadcast worldwide.

There was a separate link to the video, which I clicked on. The surgeon, wearing bloodstained scrubs, appeared at the microphone.

"The president of the European Alliance arrived at the medical wing here at the palace at 9:10 p.m.," he said. "He was unconscious and bleeding profusely, having suffered a life-threatening injury to the cranium. Our team immediately examined him for other injuries, but it was soon apparent from security personnel and our own observation that there was only one wound to which we should attend. Significant trauma had occurred to both the temporal and parietal lobes of the brain. The crushing impact of the blow to the skull was severe and unrecoverable, ultimately proving fatal. All medical personnel present in that room did our unified best"—he paused, swallowing hard—"to save the president's life, but we were unsuccessful. Official cause of death is an extensive skull fracture, resulting in an eight-inch-long intrusion into the cranial cavity itself. This was followed by massive and uncontrollable blood loss. I would add that these are preliminary remarks, and that a final analysis and conclusions will be released at a later date following an official autopsy."

Another pause.

"I would also wish to add that for myself and the other medical staff here at the palace, this is a deeply personal loss for us all. The president was . . ." The man's lip quivered, and he fought to regain his composure, before concluding, "We will all miss him."

The video ended and I closed the window, to read the rest of the report.

The presumed assassin has been identified as Hasan Ahmed Ali, a known radical Islamist, who was thought to have been killed months earlier in a coalition drone strike in Pakistan. Though there has been no official statement from the administration, an unnamed source close to the president's security detail tells Euro-Now, "The man who attacked the president is dead. He was shot multiple times by armed bodyguards. There was no attempt to save his life. He died within seconds of the attack, as he should have. There was so much blood. It's a sight that I, along with the rest of the world, will never forget."

Witnesses at the scene gave conflicting testimony regarding the sequence of events, some claiming the assassin also shouted, "Haram al-Sharif" as well as "Allahu Akbar."

"Haram al-Sharif" is an ancient reference to the Temple Mount area in Jerusalem. Some 42 months ago, following the One-Day War, the president boldly awarded the real estate containing Islam's Al Aqsā Mosque to the Jews, enraging Muslims worldwide. Since that time, there had been rumors of death threats against the president, presumably in retaliation for this decision.

I paused to reflect on what I had just read. It was no secret that the president was not favored by Muslims worldwide. After all, he had used the single stroke of a pen to deed the entire Temple Mount to the Jews, Islam's ancient enemy. What they saw as the theft and desecration of their third-holiest site gave birth to jihadist terror cells throughout Europe. Inexplicably, however, none of these cells ever materialized in public with actual attempts on the president's life. That is, until now. We may never know the assassin's precise motives or why he did not employ the typical suicide vest bomb, which would have surely killed the president, himself, and many bystanders. It is also not yet known how the attacker was able to penetrate the security bubble that perpetually insulated the president.

I suppose some questions may never be fully answered, at least to everyone's satisfaction. I brace myself for the inevitable onslaught of conspiracy theories that will surely follow. However, I suspect in the end the simplest and most sensible explanation will prove to be the most plausible one.

I was about to return my attention to the article on my phone, when the cab driver drove through a busy intersection, narrowly escaping a collision with another car. He glanced back at me in the mirror once again, this time shrugging his shoulders. I shook my head and resumed reading, hoping I would make it to the airport unscathed.

The crowd was relatively light outside the Coral House and Café Restaurant Friday evening, where the Alliance leader had been dining with members of his foreign relations cabinet. Most gathered outside were there to simply catch an up-close glimpse of the world's most popular leader.

"I can't believe my eyes," one female witness told *Euro-Now*. "I saw the attack. I was waving 'Hello, Mr. President!' when a man suddenly ran by me, holding what looked like a sword, or a large knife. Though it happened so fast, I remember noticing that he was sweating profusely, and before I could process what was happening, he swung the sword, striking the president. Then, almost immediately, the guns started firing. I naturally dropped to the ground as fast as I could." The witness added, "It's horrible. A sad day for the world. He was a great man. There will never be another like him."

The president's elite protection detail, considered to be tight, effective, and the world's best, has released no statement concerning this blatant breach of security.

Sympathetic correspondence and gestures of condolences have poured into Babylon from nations all over the world.

As we pulled in to the departure drop-off area at de Gaulle, I tucked my phone into my jacket, thanking the cab driver, who mumbled something under his breath. Once inside the busy airport, I couldn't help but notice the heightened security. Police personnel, X-ray machines, body scanners, drug-sniffing dogs, and the ever-present surveillance cameras—these were all being employed to ensure the safety of each departing flight. I suppose this could be traced to the fear that the attack on the president could be part of some larger network of terror attacks. I boarded my flight, taking my seat in 14A, and by the time we took off, I was fast asleep.

I awoke to the wheels touching down in Istanbul, where my one-hour layover passed quickly. After napping during the three-and-a-half-hour flight, I was famished, so I grabbed the first sandwich and coffee I saw upon disembarking. Big mistake, as it was the worst meal I'd eaten in recent memory. The airport was overflowing with multiple flights departing to Babylon, as it seemed the whole world was seeking passage to the ancient city. I boarded the packed plane, remaining fully awake on the Istanbul-to-Baghdad leg of my journey. I was hoping to secure something edible from the flight attendant during the course of the two-hour, fifty-five-minute flight. I must say, the onboard meal, consisting of chicken, rice, and broccoli, was considerably more to my liking.

I arrived at Baghdad International at 11:50 p.m. and was met by a driver who informed me he had been assigned to transport me to Babylon, where lodging had already been arranged. Though the president was gone, and the administration was understandably in a state of shock, it had nevertheless not suffered a loss of efficiency. The driver uttered not a word in the eighty-minute midnight ride. As I had already slept earlier, I decided to jot down some questions on my notepad, among them:

- How did someone with such a visible weapon ever get that close to the president?
- Who will provisionally, then permanently, assume the presidential duties? Will a leader from one of the participating coalition countries lobby for the appointment? Or will it be Pietro?

- How will this tragic turn of events affect the Alliance's relationships and partnerships with other nations?
- What does this mean, practically, for the Alliance itself? Will it be weakened as a result? Will it continue in its present form?
- What does all this mean for me? My work? The president's memoirs? Do I still have a job?
- Why am I, of all people, being summoned to Babylon? I am the least important person in a story like this, one with such obvious global implications.

I wrote those questions not knowing to whom I would ask them. I also still did not know the identity of the person who had sent the mysterious one-word text—Come—earlier that morning. However, I suspected I would soon find out.

We pulled up to the hotel's entrance at 1:31 a.m. My driver informed me I would be picked up at 7:30 a.m.—which meant I wouldn't be getting much sleep. I checked in, took a sleep aid, and went directly to bed.

The night passed in what seemed like moments. I awoke early, showered, dressed, and went downstairs to get a coffee and a quick breakfast before what I was sure would be a difficult day, though I still did not know my purpose for being in Babylon. The same stone-faced driver arrived outside the hotel. He immediately got out, walked around, and stood beside the sedan's rear passenger door, opening it for me when I approached. There wasn't a single parking space available in the hotel lot, further confirmation to me that Babylon was the epicenter of the world's attention at the moment. A blazing Iraqi sun greeted my eyes as I walked outside, making the car's interior, with its tinted windows, a welcomed destination.

We were just ten minutes from the palace, but my mute companion got me there in eight. As we drove up to the security gates,

I was not prepared for what I saw. Thousands had gathered outside the hilltop palace overlooking the ancient city of Babylon, presumably to mourn and pay their respects to the fallen leader. There were reporters and camera crews from TV networks and news agencies all across the world, eagerly jockeying for a vantage point from which to get a special shot of something—anything—newsworthy to broadcast. I am fairly certain they wondered who was in the darkened sedan. Little did they know how unimportant its passenger was.

After being cleared through the guard post, I was driven around the east side of the palace and dropped off under a drive-through portico. Stepping outside, I could now only faintly detect the sound of the throngs assembled on the other side and down the hill from the residence. Considering the present circumstances, it felt oddly peaceful, and the sounds of birds chirping in the trees and echoing under the portico caught my attention. An aide appeared, indicating I should follow him.

Once inside, I was led across an enormous marbled open room (I subsequently learned it was Saddam Hussein's actual former throne room). The aide opened two ornately carved wooden doors, which were easily ten to twelve feet high, and stood sentry in the doorway until I entered the room. The thick, marble walls completely insulated me from the chanting crowds outside. I found myself in a library filled with thousands of books, both ancient and modern. The smell of cedar shelves permeated the grand room, each section labeled and bordered by meticulously carved trim. I spent a few minutes perusing the vast collection of what proved to be many first-edition classics. A desk of wooden grandeur was positioned opposite the wall of shelves, behind which was a brown leather high-back chair. Facing the desk were a matching luxurious leather couch and two overstuffed chairs, with a table in between them. A thick, hardbound antiquarian book rested on the table. I picked it up and was immediately struck by its weight. I carefully opened the cover to reveal the title page. It read:

LA GUERRA
E LA PACE
LEONE TOLSTOI
VOLUME UNO
1867

I realized I was standing in the spot where the president would entertain his guests following dinner. Where drinks were toasted. Where late-night liaisons and alliances were formed. Where history was made.

Where the world was changed.

I imagined various heads of state—princes, kings, and prime ministers—who must have sat in these chairs over the past two and a half years. Words spoken here shaped the destiny of a planet in crisis. And now, it was empty and eerily silent, save for the ghostly echoes of days past. I gazed out the large window, then glanced at my watch. The time read precisely 8:30 a.m.

At that very moment, the large wooden doors slowly opened.

CHAPTER EIGHT

REVELATION IN THE LIBRARY

I turned to see the silhouette of a man standing in the doorway, his visage partially hidden by a blinding beam of light radiating through the large throne room window behind him. But when he stepped across the threshold and into the library, his identity immediately became clear.

"*Mr. President!?*" I gasped.

Tolstoy hit the marble floor with a thunderclap.

"Steady yourself, De Clercq," he replied.

"Whaa . . . How . . . you can't be . . . It's *impossible!*"

Paralyzed with shock, I was convinced my eyes were surely deceiving me. My heart rate soared while my mouth and throat became as dry as the Iraqi desert outside. I was overcome with lightheadedness and sensed the strength in my legs rapidly waning. This was a dream. It had to be. No way could this be real.

Any second now, I'm going to wake up in my hotel room, covered in sweat, I thought. *Or perhaps I have been drugged. If the president's death were indeed a part of some sinister conspiracy, then it's conceivable that his administration could have been infiltrated by subversive individuals who were accomplices to the assassin.*

I speculated that something could have been slipped into my coffee at the hotel, and I was having some sort of psychotropic experience. At the moment, I could not know this for certain, but one thing I *did* know for sure—something that was undeniable—the president was dead! I knew that. Why, everyone in the world knew it. So there had to be some other bizarre explanation for what I was seeing and hearing, and dreams and drugs were as good as any!

The human figure in my hallucination began slowly walking toward me, as if gliding on air.

"Julien, do not be afraid. It's really me. You are not dreaming," he said, smiling.

His words hit me like an invisible train, propelling me backward and causing me to fall into the overstuffed chair behind me. Pronounced chills ran all over my skin, as if they had taken root in my very nervous system. I could hear the sound of my heart pounding in my chest. The room suddenly grew uncharacteristically cold. I swallowed hard in an effort to moisten my arid throat.

"What's going on here?" I inquired, looking around the room for answers. "Where am I? Who are you?"

The man came closer and sat opposite me in an identical chair.

"Relax, my friend. Everything will be explained to you."

Once again, I frantically scanned the room, looking for some clue that would tell me whether I was actually in the palace library or merely pinned to this chair, paralyzed and trapped in some surreal nightmare. Sweat beaded on my brow, defying the sudden chill in the room.

"Julien, look at me," he said forcefully. "Look at my head."

Transferring my focus away from his captivating gaze, I followed his pointing finger. Clearly visible on the left side of his head was a thin, narrow cavity just above his ear. Beginning at his temple, it extended rearward, disappearing somewhere behind his left ear. The entire side of his skull was disfigured. His hair had been partially shaved in that area, and numerous stitches ran the length of the gash. He noticed me staring at it.

"That's what they did to me in the trauma room here at the palace Friday night, stitching me up after declaring me dead. And I *was* dead, Julien. No heartbeat. No detectable brain activity. And why not? For what other fate could possibly await someone suffering such a mortal wound? The fracturing of my skull caused by the penetration of the steel blade into my brain alone was sufficient to cause my demise. This, along with the enormous loss of blood, both at the scene and afterward here in the trauma room, was validating proof to every doctor present that I was indeed *dead*. But you didn't need a degree in medicine to verify that. It was an undeniable fact.

"It was in all their best interests to save my life that night, or at least keep me alive somehow. But they were unable. There was nothing they, or any other mortal man, could do. Death's dark hand had visited me in that hour, taking hold of me with an inescapable grip. I was gone. And therefore, officially pronounced dead. That was their consensus then, and it's their belief even now, some thirty-five hours later."

"But that's simply not possible," I interjected, beginning to feel a modicum of lucidity return to me. "How could you . . . You look so alive, and apparently with no pain . . ."

"Your initial shock and disbelief are understandable. It's natural and expected. And your awestruck response is but the first among billions." He let out a slight laugh. "Truthfully, had it not happened to me, I, too, would have difficulty accepting it. But allow me to elaborate a bit and tell you what I remember over these last three days."

Julien, I said to myself, *are you sure this is really happening?* I was still questioning my own ability to distinguish between perception and reality. *Should I be writing this down? Or recording it?* But I had brought no recorder, pen, or pad. I saw no need to. But these proved to be inconsequential thoughts, as the president's every word was mind-stamped into my head, chiseled indelibly into my memory.

"I vividly remember leaving Coral House Restaurant Friday evening," he said, "accompanied by two staff members and my security detail. Then I heard a noise, and out of my periphery, I detected the figure of a man, arm raised and a swordlike object in his hand. He ran toward me, swinging, and I instinctively ducked. As it turns out, however, not quite enough, for his sword struck me"—he pointed to the side of his head—"here, as you can plainly see. I briefly recall a severe, stinging sensation, the likes of which I had never known. And then my memory goes dark."

He slowly leaned forward, lowering his voice as if he were about to tell me a secret.

"This is where the story may get a bit uncomfortable for you, Julien. Maybe even disturbing, at least initially. And I want you to listen very closely to what I am about to tell you."

What could be any more unbelievable than what I have already *seen and heard?* I reasoned. "I am listening, sir."

He leaned even closer.

"In spite of every lifesaving procedure and all the medical training known to man, my body ceased to function, causing my death sometime Friday evening between the time of the initial attack and when I was here in the palace. I expired on a gurney not one hundred feet from where you and I now sit. *I was dead.* There was absolutely no doubt of this in the minds of every doctor present. In fact, I am told that three separate physicians examined me to confirm this fact. And every news outlet in the world has now accurately reported it.

"I left this body, and this world. And yet, strangely enough, in death my consciousness did not cease to function. I was still very aware. Thinking. Processing. Even emoting. I don't know where I was, but a familiar voice inside told me I was not alone in that place. I was not frightened or confused. On the contrary, I felt oddly comforted in my new state of consciousness. In fact, I even felt emboldened and empowered. Time was not measured during this altered state of postmortem awareness. I existed in the eternal present, surrounded by nothingness. This went on for an unknown period of time. The next thing I remember, I slowly opened my eyes, discovering myself in my own bed here at the palace, with Pietro sitting by my side.

"'Welcome back, sir,' he said with a smile. 'And this time, never to die again.'

"As I rose and sat up in my bed, I felt possessed by an enlightenment I had never known before. It was as if the world had been reborn right before me, and I before it. I no longer perceived myself as a mere man, but *more* than one. *For what ordinary man,* I asked myself, *comes back from the dead? Who can conquer the grave and defeat mankind's most formidable foe?*"

Still leaning forward, he raised his eyebrows. "Who, indeed?" Then he rested back into the chair.

I was absorbing his words, taking them at face value, for I had no preconceived template or filter through which to read them. He continued.

"Thoughts of grandeur dominated me as I awoke, thoughts that heretofore had not existed. I suddenly became aware of a new stewardship within me. I felt infused with the wisdom of a hundred lifetimes and leaders, as if I were both Nebuchadnezzar *and* Napoleon. I cannot trace for you the source of this glorious embodiment of knowledge. I only know that it now resides in me.

"Without education, counsel, or conversation, I intuitively knew that simply leading the European Alliance can no longer suffice for me. It's clear now that the scope of my previous rule suffered from shortsightedness, limited by my own human ego and unrealistic notions of world peace. I have led the world as a man would. I appealed, cajoled, and negotiated. I was a diplomat. I accepted and tolerated refusals to comply and unite with me. I patiently waited for the nations to see the light. I promised peace and brought calm to their chaos, when I should have done so while demanding their unwavering loyalty. I allowed diplomacy to dictate too many of my policies and procedures. As a result, I now lament the lenience of days past, and pledge to henceforth forge a new path of unity through strength, without allowance for dissent."

I listened intently, now convinced it truly was the president, the man I had come to know, who was physically seated across from me. It was his voice, his face. His personality. And yet, energized with an unfamiliar spirit. And the look in his eyes told me he believed every word coming out of his mouth.

I remained seated deep in the overstuffed chair, as if pinned there by an unseen hand. My initial shock and wonder at seeing the president alive had only mildly subsided. I was still mentally and emotionally transitioning out of this thick cloud of disbelief. I was no longer in outright denial, but rather now attempted to reconcile what my brain told me was real with what my other senses were telling me. I searched my mind, endeavoring to find some precedent in my own life, or another's, to which I could compare this experience. But there was none. This phenomenon was unique in my lifetime, or in anyone's as far as I knew. A trickle of sweat snaked its way down my back. I was sure the president noticed how nervous I was. I kept my hands glued to my knees, to prevent them from visibly shaking.

"Sir, it's really *you*!? I mean . . . if I may ask, how do you . . . we . . . explain all this? The world will want to know. They'll want answers. This will be the biggest story, news, event since, well . . . since *ever*!"

He did not hesitate with his answer.

"We will simply tell them the truth, of course. I am alive! And from there, many things will naturally progress."

His response made sense, for what else *would* one do in an extraordinary circumstance such as this? Yes, just tell the truth. But this particular truth was so unbelievable. And yet, there it was, sitting in the chair opposite me. Still, I was unable to wrap my head around what had happened, or what was currently happening in my presence. Mine was a mind in conflict. I wanted to believe. I *did* believe. But I had never been one to embrace the mystical or supernatural in my thirty-one years of living. And this situation screamed both. I had always reasoned that faith in something greater or "Someone up there" was for the emotionally weak or the intellectually deficient, and I considered myself neither. However, I concluded that this belief in what was a physically verifiable, historical event wasn't really faith at all, but rather merely mental assent to an undeniable fact. And the reason for my justification for believing in the supernatural in this case was that it wasn't some ancient story passed down through the ages, but rather something I could see, hear, and touch. I was an eyewitness, not a man who took someone else's word as truth. Like believing in the visible, known laws of biology and science, the only difference being that this incident transcended those very laws! In those few minutes alone with my president, I will admit, my mind passed through a portal of sorts.

I now believed in miracles.

"So, what's next, sir? And what's my role? How do I fit into all this?"

I wiped my sweaty palms on my pants. No doubt, the president could tell I was now convinced he was a risen man.

"Julien, your job now becomes even more critical. The story you have been writing just got exponentially more interesting, wouldn't you say?"

"Oh, yes! Without a doubt!" I agreed.

"You will continue chronicling my legacy, but now more as my official scribe than my ghost biographer. I am permanently assigning you to Babylon. You will relocate here immediately and accompany my entourage whenever I travel. We'll arrange to have your things sent here from Brussels."

"That-that's fine, sir. I'll be happy to be here and to keep writ—"

"There is one more thing, Julien," he broke in. "Something that's necessary before proceeding."

"Yes, sir?"

"I want you to come over here," he paused briefly, as his eyes locked on mine, "and touch it."

"T-touch it, sir? Touch what?" I asked.

He turned his head slightly to my left.

"My wound," he explained. "I want you to come here and see that it is truly me. Put your hand on my head and know it is real. Know. Believe. And do not ever doubt."

I said nothing, but simply stood and walked around the table separating our two chairs. Again, he tilted his head, exposing his wound to me. I gradually lifted my still-trembling right hand and gently touched the side of his head and the hideous scar marking him. I then quickly withdrew it, as if I had come in contact with a hot object. He was real. The wound was real. I had felt it. I believed.

"All right," he said. "Now, we have much to do, and little time to accomplish it. The crowds outside, along with the world press, have gathered and are anxiously awaiting an official statement from my administration concerning Friday's assassination. Naturally, they expect Pietro to make the announcement. They do not know that it is I who will ascend the platform. Accompanying me will be the same attending physicians who verified my death. And by now they have all signed sworn statements to that effect. But before hearing from them, I will address the world, assuring them of my rebirth from the dead. They will know they now have a leader who cannot be defeated, one who will lead them into a thousand years of peace and prosperity."

He stood from his chair, extending his hand, and I obliged. His grip was firm, but this time more than that. It was authoritative and dominant. I could feel my head slowly tilt forward, bowing before him in humility. In awe. It felt appropriate. Natural.

He accepted my adoration. "Come now, Julien. They're waiting."

"I just need to visit the toilet for a moment, if I may, sir."

"Of course. Join me in the great hall, at the main entrance in five minutes."

And with that, he turned and exited the library, the wooden doors having anticipated his arrival and opened from the other side. I bent down and lifted Tolstoy from the marble floor, placing the book back on the table. I wondered what a great writer like him would say about all this. Entering the WC, I went straightway to the sink. The beads of sweat were prominent on my brow, and though the library seemed eerily cold, perspiration had soaked my shirt during my conversation with the president. I splashed my face with water, staring into the mirror and once again confirming this was reality and not some delusional dreamscape conjured up by my sleeping subconscious. The cold water on my face helped authenticate my belief. This *was* really happening. With the water still dripping off my face, I spoke to my image in the mirror, "Julien, old boy, how did *you* get *here*?" I dried my face and straightened my disheveled shirt. "Okay," I heard the man in the mirror say. "Here we go."

I exited the toilet and picked up my pace to join the company of individuals who were now surrounding the president. The all-male contingency of some twenty or so were busy shaking his hand, congratulating him and praising him for his incomprehensible, supernatural accomplishment. And to a man, each of them instinctively bowed his head before him, just as I had felt compelled to do. I noticed that his wound looked considerably less gory than it had in the library just minutes earlier. Pietro stood to his right, looking satisfied and eager, his blue eyes made even more piercing by the brightly lit hall. As I arrived at the outer edge of this circle of adulation, he acknowledged me, smiling with a slight nod.

"Good to see you received my text," he said.

So it was him, I concluded.

"Are we all ready?" the president inquired.

There was a collective murmur of assent.

"Then let's go."

The enormous, decorative wooden doors were opened by two uniformed soldiers, and the president stepped into the morning light. Temporary barricades had been put in place, ensuring a safe distance between the throngs of people and the platform, which was erected atop the large terrace in front of the palace's front entrance. Security was at an all-time high, with additional agents stationed in a protective semicircle around the newly erected stage. The gradual slope descending from the palatial residence was filled with mourners and spectators from all parts of the world. Some had made signs, even banners, eulogizing their fallen prince. I guessed there were more than ten thousand gathered there.

And then they saw him.

Gasps erupted throughout the crowd, along with rippling shrieks of fear, as they recognized their once-dead Alliance leader. A wave of confusing chatter began to swell, growing louder. And before he even reached the stage, the president raised both fists triumphantly into the air, pumping them heavenward. A thunderous roar blasted from the thousands assembled, as if a last-second goal had won them the World Cup. Their cheers reverberated onto the plain below, echoing throughout the rebuilt streets of ancient Babylon.

We followed the president as he ascended the steps of the elevated platform. With fists still raised high, he strutted to the microphone wearing a victorious grin.

"Good morning!" he shouted.

Many began jumping up and down, exuberantly embracing one another. They had likely never seen the president in person before. So, in light of this occasion, their sight of him now was even more meaningful and memorable.

He lowered his fists and gripped the sides of the podium.

"To all citizens of the Alliance, to all foreign leaders, to those from nations watching around the world, and to the privileged ones assembled here today, *I greet you!*"

A renewed celebratory ovation burst from the crowd, lasting at least a minute. The president savored the moment, clapping as he paced back and forth from one side of the stage to the other. He then returned to the microphone.

"Two days ago, I was the victim of a vicious assault at the hands of a crazed assassin."

The massive audience fell silent as the miracle man spoke.

"This individual we now believe was part of a larger terrorist network bent on seeking revenge for my advances toward world peace . . . *your* peace. In that attack, I was struck on the side of the head with a large sword. The sword penetrated my skull, fracturing it in several places. It then entered into my cranial cavity, impacting my brain. The damage was severe—and fatal. Despite efforts by the finest trauma physicians and surgeons, there was nothing any of them could do. I died that evening, as attested to by my medical team, who join me here today."

The five doctors assembled behind him all nodded their heads, solemnly affirming his words.

Sporadic expletives were heard coming from the crowd, as well as more articulate expressions of wonder, shock, and fear.

I was standing behind him to his left, when something very curious caught my attention. The prominent scar left by the sword and subsequent stitching was gradually disappearing! Only minutes earlier, it had been undeniably visible. I had both seen and touched it! Yet now, all that could be seen was a faint, hairline anomaly just above his left ear. He was healing before our very eyes, and at a startling, unprecedented rate. He really was the "Miracle Man"!

He went on.

"It was written by the ancient Greeks that 'death is a common fate among humanity, and eventually comes to us all.' And we can all attest to this, having seen billions disappear or die these past forty-two months. That dark shroud which ends our lives is an intimidating enemy, defeated by no mere man. But when death came for *me*, I want you to know it was confronted by a worthy adversary, and one who refused to be vanquished by it!"

Another round of deafening applause and cheering broke out. The president motioned for silence before continuing.

"Now, I cannot stand here today and fully explain what happened to me during the days after my heart ceased to beat, and when my brain no longer displayed activity. I can only say that I left this mortal, material world, and was led to the mythological rivers of my Roman ancestors. There, I was bid to drink from the waters of forgetfulness, and to leave all memory of this life upon entering the next."

Wow. He didn't mention this part to me in the library, I said to myself.

"But I resolutely rejected death's offer. Instead, I turned from my journey toward Elysium, and resolutely began making my way back to life here . . . with *you*. It was there I encountered that dreaded supernatural centurion of death."

There was hardly a sound on the hillside as he spoke, the massive crowd having gone silent in his presence. The only noise was the faint chirping of birds, as if celebrating this new day with their own voices.

"Standing there face-to-face, I drew a sword of my own—the double-edged sword of Determination and Self-Reliance. Wielding it forward, I struck a mortal blow, slaying the death angel in his own domain! My friends, the grave, though real, only temporarily held sway over me. *Behold, I was dead. but now I am alive!*"

He shouted these words, his fists again raised high in the air. The legion of fans and followers broke into an ovation of chants lasting several minutes. The president stood proud, looking over the crowd, smiling, and soaking it in. This momentous gathering had all the earmarks of a political rally or victory party. But it was something more. Much more. We were there, not to mourn the passing of a diplomat, but to celebrate the resurrection of a deity. At least, that's what it seemed like. It was in the air. No one said it at the time. No one had to. It was just mutually, simultaneously understood. We were witnessing a supernatural phenomenon. Something defying human explanation.

Once more, he motioned for quiet. A hush fell over the multitude.

"Momentarily, my medical team and security commissioner will come forward to answer any questions you may have regarding my attack and the attacker, who I am pleased to say was promptly cut down by gunfire at the scene—I am quite certain that he will *not* overcome death," he added, prompting laughter and applause from the crowd.

"Now, I want both the news media as well as citizens all over the earth to be well-informed regarding what has transpired. You will be provided unlimited access to view actual footage of the assassination and hear eyewitness accounts we have compiled. Even so, there will be skeptics, naysayers, rebels—those who refuse to believe what has happened here."

A wave of boos and hisses leaked from the crowd.

"Yes, they may refuse to believe in *me*. But I have every confidence that they will eventually be persuaded. Some may call me a martyr, a victim of leadership in a divisive global climate. But you can save your laments for those who die for some temporal, noble cause. Let me be clear. I am not a victim, but rather, the *victor*!"

Another frenzied cheer arose from the outdoor assembly.

"I see all those who dwell on earth now as *my* citizens, *my* people. Regardless of our past differences and divisions, we can now unite under a common banner for global good. Unite under *me*, and just as I defeated death, I will defeat what threatens you, giving you what you need to survive and to lead lives of great fulfillment.

"And lastly, I didn't simply come back from the grave as a once-dead man. No. I have returned with *power* and *authority*. And I have conferred that power upon my faithful minister of affairs, Pietro Moretti. He is my most trusted advocate. My right hand. My mouthpiece. My *prophet*. When he speaks, I speak. When he acts, he does so with my full approval and authority. Hear him as you would me. Obey him as if he *were* me."

Looking over his shoulder, he motioned. "Pietro, come forward and give a demonstration of our strength."

The man in whom resided the president's explicit trust stepped up to the microphone, and without hesitation raised one arm toward the heavens. "Behold," he said, "in the name of the one who now wears the mantles of both Nimrod and Nebuchadnezzar, I command you to come forth!"

At those words, there was a deep rumbling beneath our feet and on the distant plain. Then was heard a deafening clap of thunder, after which from the sky came a blinding column of light, as if made of fire. It descended in a flash, touching down near us in the old city of Babylon. The surrounding desert was even further illuminated by its brilliance. Everyone covered their eyes, as we were awestruck at the sight of this miracle. And as if choreographed, the massive, multinational crowd was instantly gripped with fear, whereupon they spontaneously fell to their knees, bowing toward the platform upon which the president stood. News cameras were splintered in their coverage, some focusing on the pillar of fire, some on the crowds, and others on the man who had come back from the grave.

Pietro lowered his arm, and the fire instantly retreated back into the sky, leaving behind a blackened crater in the scorched earth. The president waved to the crowd, spanning from left to right, while cameras recorded more footage from the event. Incidentally, that morning's global broadcast constituted the largest viewing audience in history. The president then motioned to his medical and security teams to take the stage for questions from the media.

On that Sunday morning in Babylon, and in that moment, my heart became paralyzed with an indescribable fear, one I had never known. It was a sobering sense of dread, really. I awoke, had coffee, and then minutes later met a man who had risen from the dead. Not your ordinary day. For me, truth and reality had suddenly been redefined. I remember thinking to myself, *Who is this man? Who is like him? And if death cannot defeat him, who is there who can win against him?* My insides were churning, so I hurriedly and covertly stepped behind a palm tree and vomited breakfast. I emerged feeling only somewhat relieved, only to discover the president himself standing but a few feet away, smiling and gazing at me with his penetrating stare. He motioned me to come, I walked toward him, and we were joined by Pietro. The three of us retreated back into the palace residence.

"Have you spoken with the general?" he asked his minister of affairs.

"Yes, sir," he replied. "He is at the location, on standby and waiting for your command."

"Excellent. Then let's proceed."

Standing next to them, I felt like a fish out of water. "Sir, what would you like me to do now?" I asked.

"You'll come with me, Julien," he answered. "Just listen, observe, and remember what you see."

"May I ask, wh-where are we going?"

His response was blunt.

"Jerusalem. We have business in Jerusalem."

CHAPTER NINE

JERUSALEM

Ben Gurion Airport is located just forty-eight kilometers north-west of Jerusalem, and our flight time from Babylon was approximately one hour and forty-five minutes. On board the plane was the president, Pietro, four high-ranking military personnel, and me. As my proximity to the president didn't include sitting in on high-level staff meetings, I again sat alone in a row of empty seats. Having traveled directly from the palace to the administration's airfield in Babylon, this left me no time to return to my hotel and retrieve my writing materials. I asked one of the stewards for a pen and some paper, and was soon provided a notepad bearing the presidential seal. I spent the entire flight time jotting down in meticulous detail everything I had seen and heard that morning. I will admit, even as I wrote, it still felt like fiction. But I had witnessed it firsthand and could attest to its accuracy.

Once we touched down in Israel and taxied to a stop, we disembarked and boarded an awaiting helicopter for the short trip to Jerusalem. The helicopter was employed to avoid any unnecessary security risks on the ground. I sat opposite the president and

Pietro and reopened the bottle of water I had been nursing on the plane. They were reviewing some documents in a folder, when the president paused, peering over the top of his seldom-used reading glasses.

"Julien, we realize today's events have been both shocking and surprising to you. Perhaps even traumatic."

My trembling hand must have given me away . . . that and the fact that I had vomited on palace grounds. I swallowed.

"I want to assure you that you are safe and have nothing to fear, either from myself or from Pietro here. But you must know that not everyone will accept this miracle that has happened to me. Outside of an expected level of disbelief and skepticism, there will be scattered acts of rebellion, some possibly becoming violent. And we will deal with those as they arise. First and foremost, however, know that I am protected here, not just by my personal security and military guard, but also by a force not of this world. As you have seen and will see, my administration and agenda have become empowered and accompanied by the supernatural. It's not something I am able to fully explain to you, nor do I need to. Keep your eyes open and you will have all the explanation you'll need. But the point is that because we cannot be touched, therefore neither can you. You fall directly under my personal umbrella of protection and security."

I was unsure how to respond, so I just nodded, indicating that I understood. He put his pen down and closed the folder, his attention even more focused on me.

"Julien, from this point on, things are going to be . . ." He glanced sideways at his political partner. "They're going to be *intensified*. Because of what we have to accomplish, certain extreme measures will be necessary, especially in the launch stage of our future economic vision. I tell you this, my trusted young friend, because you sit in a highly privileged position. And also because I don't want you to be alarmed or caught off guard, thus detracting from your ability to effectively do your job. You will need to detach yourself somewhat from your feelings and insulate your mind from unproductive thoughts. Remember, I did not hire you to editorialize or insert your opinions, but rather to accurately record, from my perspective, the legacy of my administration and reign."

"I completely understand, sir. I will do exactly as you say," I replied, though not really understanding what he meant. I thought about asking him to elaborate, but I reasoned that things would naturally unfold, becoming clear to me in time. I just didn't realize at the time how soon that would be.

He reopened the folder, and he and Pietro resumed their previous conversation. Looking out the helicopter window, I saw below that we were being shadowed by a military convoy, including a dozen armored vehicles with mounted turret guns. I counted them. I also could hear the whir of additional helicopters and the roar of jets streaking over us. This was definitely not going to be a diplomatic visit. But why would any military force be necessary in light of what I'd seen Pietro do earlier that morning? This obviously wasn't my concern. I wasn't there to question, but to document. Just keep my ears and eyes open. And write it down. Simple.

As we began descending, I could see a crowd was already forming. Armed Alliance soldiers were surrounding the location, which I immediately recognized. Though the sound of rotors prevented me from hearing, the large assembly on the ground was shouting and chanting something.

The president closed his folder and handed it to one of the uniformed army officers. He turned to Pietro. "You're certain all the necessary preparations have been made?"

"Everything is prepared and in order, sir. We're ready."

With the blades still turning, the helicopter's door was opened by a member of the security team, and immediately a platoon of soldiers appeared, snapping to attention. The president exited the aircraft, followed by Pietro, the officers, and then me. The president acknowledged the soldiers, then turned toward the distant, chanting crowds and smiled. The entourage proceeded across the stone pavement toward the Jewish temple.

The grand edifice's construction over three years ago was made possible by the president's savvy mediation following the Russian-Muslim War against Israel. I say "mediation," but in reality, he essentially commandeered this highly esteemed portion of Jerusalem real esate from the Muslims, giving it back to Israel by executive order, acting as if it were his to give. The Islamic world had little recourse following the previous decimation of their national military forces worldwide. The Islamic religious group (or waqf) who had formerly managed their mosque at the Temple Mount had no choice but to sign the historic peace accord. In truth, for the Muslims, it was their own eviction notice disguised as a peace agreement. And they had signed it!

As we entered the outer temple area, there was a brief pause for the Alliance soldiers to get into formation. I still had no idea as to the nature of the president's visit here. Was he here to receive an award? Or perhaps follow up with those Jews with whom he had been so gracious? If so, then why the military presence? Every eye in the crowd was fixated on him who, just days ago, was cut down by an assassin's blade. Some cheered while others held their hands over their mouths in disbelief.

Suddenly, without warning, a command was given, and the soldiers readied their rifles, pointing them at the temple priests and attendants who were present. The president and his minister of affairs began walking toward the outermost door when one of the priests scurried ahead of them, blocking the entrance.

"What's the meaning of this?" he inquired. "The temple is not—"

Before he could complete his sentence, he was summarily shot in the head right where he stood. I recoiled at the sound of the rifle's report. High-pitched screams burst from the crowd, sending men and women scattering in every direction.

The president calmly stepped over the priest's lifeless body and continued into the outer courtyard. A squad of soldiers accompanied him while several more remained outside to contain a growing contingency of Jews who rushed up to begin protesting what they saw as an unwarranted breach of the temple gate. I trailed behind the president, Pietro, and the army unit. As they made their way into the inner courtyard, they encountered other priests, attendants, and a few animals. Before being given the chance to protest or question this unorthodox invasion of their temple, they were all shot and killed on sight, their blood seeping into the porous rock pavement. Lampstands and altars were then toppled.

Two soldiers then ran up the steps leading to the entrance of the main building and opened the huge, gold-plated double doors. The presidential party entered the main sanctuary, where several wide-eyed, aged priests also met their deaths. The president's face was the last thing any of them saw. That, and the barrel of a gun.

It goes without saying, I was once again traumatized. The sight of so much blood alone was making me queasy and light-headed. I could not conceive of what offense these Jewish priests must have committed to justify such brutal executions. But I was certain there had to be information regarding these extreme measures of which I was unaware. It was becoming a brutal slaughter.

With every Jewish male within my range of sight either dead or dying, there remained yet one place in the temple the president's feet had yet to tread: the odd chamber that Jews consider most sacred. They called it the "Holy of Holies," and deep within its thick stone walls was housed a very peculiar relic. It was a large box-shaped object, an antiquity from their past. This magnificently carved chest was overlaid with pure gold, on top of which sat two bizarre-looking angelic creatures, their heads bowed and their wings touching each other's. When they told me its name, I remembered hearing of it. The "ark of the covenant" was the subject of much myth and superstition, having been depicted in various movies of the last century.

But there was more fact than folklore regarding this revered Jewish trophy. I later conducted some research and discovered that the ark had gone missing centuries ago after King Nebuchadnezzar of Babylon destroyed Jerusalem in 586 BCE. Jewish tradition claims the temple at that time, having been built by their king, Solomon, included secret underground vaults and passageways running beneath the temple area. The legend also asserts that temple priests stealthily carried the ark deep into one of these chambers to hide it from the invading Babylonian king.

Upon further study, I also discovered that the rebuilt temple standing during the time of Jesus had no ark in its holy place. It was believed by some that when Nebuchadnezzar's army ransacked the temple, they removed the ark along with hundreds of other temple valuables and artifacts. Another theory was that when the Babylonians arrived, they found that the ark was already gone. This latter version is corroborated by the Jews who rebuilt this most recent temple. Having had no temple for some two thousand years, the Jews were very eager to rebuild their sacred structure just as it had been in Solomon's day.

After the Muslim Dome was demolished three and a half years ago, Israeli excavations were done and thermographic readings were taken, revealing large pockets of air underneath an area adjacent to the location of the Holy of Holies. During one dig, Jewish archaeological teams discovered a series of mazelike passageways, ultimately leading to a room containing a very dusty but intact ark of the covenant! Hidden away for centuries, but never forgotten, it remained reasonably unblemished and un-deteriorated, having been constructed of nearly indestructible acacia wood and, of course, gold. This historic discovery only heightened the Jewish people's motivation to aggressively begin construction of their temple in record time. To be honest, I was eager to see what it looked like with my own eyes.

However, the ark was not immediately visible, as separating the Holy of Holies from the larger outer room was a very high, thick curtain, which served as an entranceway into this most sacred of all Jewish places. The president motioned with his hand, and a squad of soldiers ran forward and violently jerked the giant curtain, which collapsed onto the stone floor. What was revealed behind it was a rare sight for human eyes. In fact, the Jewish high priest only saw it once a year while performing his ritualistic duties. And as I previously mentioned, no one had beheld it for some 2,600 years. For fifteen to twenty seconds, every person gazing upon that religious relic stood motionless. Perhaps no other mortal treasure, religious or secular, commanded as much awe as that one ancient object. Maybe the Grail of Christ would come close, but it, too, had been lost to the ages. The light of the room brilliantly reflected off the gleaming, pure gold. That which had for so long been hidden from the world was now exposed. The Jews believed the actual presence of their God dwelt above that golden chest. But upon its revelation, no one present there that day saw him. No smoke. No fire. No "glory cloud." And no supernatural lasers of judgment emanating from it.

Just a gold box sitting in silent seclusion.

Everyone held their ground while the president slowly and deliberately stepped forward, until at last, he stood before the large object. Reaching forward with both hands, he took hold of the golden angels' wings, which met over the center of the ark. He then began bending them backward, until at last he had created a space between them large enough for a person to occupy. Whirling back toward those present, he announced with a loud voice, "This place where I am standing is believed by the Jews to be reserved for God alone. Therefore, it is only fitting that God should take his seat here!" And with that, he lifted himself up, ascending on top of the ark, and took his seat in the Jews' holiest place. By doing so, he had officially desecrated their temple, and he knew it. But he had also effectively expelled their God as well. Years ago, he had tossed out the Muslims from this very spot. Minutes ago, he had removed the priestly Jewish representatives. And now, the ultimate coup d'état, he had unseated their God's symbolic presence as well.

The thirty or so soldiers who had witnessed this action gazed at him, and then at one another, with some measure of confusion. I assume they were unsure as to the meaning of his actions, whether they were meant to be symbolic or real. But the president wasn't yet finished with his speech. Still smugly seated upon the ark like an Olympian who had just won gold, he loosened his tie. "Tell me. Why should anyone worship a God he cannot see?" he thundered. "And why would a religion of any worth hide their God behind a curtain? Are they ashamed of him? Listen to me. He is no God who sits idly alone all day long waiting for animals to be butchered for his perverse pleasure. Absurd! A true deity is not so apathetic, but rather takes action! He clearly demonstrates why there are to be no other gods before him. The Jews call the place where I now sit the 'mercy seat.' Ha! No. No. On this day, I am declaring it to be MY seat, a seat of *judgment*! From this moment forward, this temple belongs to *me*. It is *my* 'holy place'!"

He turned to his minister of affairs and grinned. Pietro grinned back.

"This is where *my* presence will dwell in perpetuity," the president roared. "No more sacrifices. No more feasts. No more Sabbath. And no more Jews. Did you hear that, Israel? Your God is dead . . . and so are you!"

With those words, repeated gunfire was heard outside, followed by riotous, horror-filled cries. The temple—and the area that surrounded it—suddenly became a slaughterhouse, with hundreds of Israeli citizens being executed, much like the temple animals that were slaughtered in days gone by. More troops began pouring into the city, entering homes and businesses to carry out the orders of him who had proved himself to be God by rising from the dead. There was not a corner of that ancient city, Jerusalem, untouched by terror and trails of blood. The wailing was unceasing. Scores of residents were seen fleeing from the city and into the surrounding wilderness in hopes of escaping the wrath of him who sat in the holy place.

As for me, I can only say that all my life I had taken great pride in being an independent self-thinker. I have never been religious, nor were my parents. Religion was not a large part of my culture either. As a result, I was mostly agnostic in my thinking and life philosophy. Mankind was all there was, and that was it. But I could not deny what I witnessed on that day, and I became fully convinced that this president was indeed more than just a man. How that was possible, I could not explain. What I had seen defied all human reasoning, and yet his claims and assertions had been validated, both by convincing signs and wonders, and by his own supernatural return from the grave.

I was a believer.

My mind drifted back to that first day in Rome, when I was mesmerized by the Nicolas Poussin painting of the destruction of the Jewish temple. Was that an eerie foreshadowing of what was to come? Or perhaps the president had intentionally displayed it there as inspiration. When did he first imagine this terrible day of desecration? I would never know.

The self-proclaimed deity eventually hopped down from his newly claimed golden throne. There was a fearless swagger in his

INTERVIEW WITH THE ANTICHRIST

step. He casually strolled past the uniformed soldiers and Pietro, walking directly toward me.

At this point, four more soldiers approached, dragging two odd-looking old men. Clothed in what I later discovered were coarse black goat-hair garments, they also wore long beards and were obviously Jews. Upon being presented to the president, their identities were revealed. These men were Israeli street preachers, who, for more than three years, had gained sizable notoriety through their barbaric appearance and public proclamations about matters relating to their religion, temple sacrifices, and their long-awaited Messiah. Now, that by itself was only a minor irritant to the president, as they had primarily kept themselves within the bounds of the Temple area and the borders of Jerusalem. But over time, their sermons grew increasingly hostile, including vitriolic, damnable rants against the president and his administration. This angered Alliance loyalists in Jerusalem, who also blamed the two for some of the catastrophes that had befallen the earth. Like they were "bad luck" to the planet. Various attempts on their lives were made in an effort to shut them up and to prevent them from bringing additional mayhem.

However, they managed to survive and cheat death, a feat some credited to divine intervention and supernatural acts, like real fire proceeding from their mouths. Such fantastical rumors not having been substantiated, nevertheless, here they now stood, facing the end of their preaching careers.

"You two," the president sneered. He cut his eyes toward the soldiers, prompting a coordinated kick to the backs of their legs, sending them to their knees.

"Thaaat's better. Now you're where you belong. So, these are the infamous troublemakers, huh? I have looked forward to meeting you both."

The one on the right defiantly shot back, "It is you who are the troublemaker of Israel, O insolent king."

136

His words immediately triggered a rifle butt's blast to his mouth.

"Silence, *Jew*!" the soldier barked.

Blood began pouring from his lips, flowing down into his gray beard.

"Enough of this!" the president announced. "You had your day. Preaching. Praying. Prophesying. But all that ends right here, right now. You know, I actually feel sorry for you—a pitiful, misguided race of people of whom the world has finally had enough. You have spent over three years gathering followers and garnering attention for yourselves. Well, if it is the spotlight you crave, then I shall give it to you. But before I let you go, know this: yours is a dead religion . . . and so are you!"

And with that, another soldier stepped forward wielding a dagger, and swiftly cut the prophets' throats. The two lifeless bodies hit the stone pavement with a dull thud, their blood intermingling with that of their previously slain brethren.

The president once again turned his attention toward me.

"What do you think of all this, Julien De Clercq? I am curious to know your mind."

At first, I was unable to speak. His eyes were locked on mine with a commanding stare. I was beginning to realize I was no longer just an employee, or even a privileged inner-circle observer. Rather, my identity was changing as I became overwhelmed with a deep sense of unworthiness in his presence. I was now subservient. My will had been vanquished by his. And standing there, I could tell he knew it.

I fell to my knees, physically acknowledging my undying adulation and full devotion to him. Bowing before him on that warm temple pavement, I surrendered myself to him. For the first time since childhood, I could feel tears escaping from my eyes. And as they stained the stone below me, I felt his hand on my head.

"Rise, Julien."

I slowly stood, my tear-filled eyes still blurred. Consumed by awe, reverence, and fear—and with the echoing cries of terror and death resounding in the distance—I heard him speak.

"You are cognizant of who I am now. That's good. And you have come to this knowledge because of what you have seen and heard, and also because your heart is open and your mind is untainted by lies. Up to this point, you have been merely a keen observer and a collector of facts. But now, you are a believer and a worshiper. This is a natural and appropriate response."

"I am honored to be one of your servants, sir," I confessed, slowly standing. "But may I ask something?" Looking around at the death and devastation inside the temple, I humbly asked, "What necessitated all this? And I don't mean to question you, but aren't the Jews a peace-loving people? Haven't they kept to themselves, like you said they would, quietly going about their business and attending to their religion? What did they do to deserve today's harsh measures?"

The corner of his mouth turned up, forming a smirk. Then, just as suddenly, his visage turned somber.

"Allow me to connect the dots for you, Julien. Ever since the great vanishing almost four years ago, the mass of humanity has searched for meaning and purpose in the midst of confusion and chaos. Shortly after that time, as you recall, we established a global religious network, which allowed people from a vast number of faith persuasions and beliefs to come together and express themselves however they deemed appropriate. This was necessary in order to placate their need for something greater, and also provide a solace for their misery and suffering. It temporarily numbed their pain.

"But now we are in a different day. Now is the time for true unity. We can no longer survive as a race if we are splintered in a thousand different religious directions. It is time for the world to converge into one faith. One religion, and one object of worship. I AM that object of worship. Others will readily jettison their former beliefs, religions, and superstitions once they see who I am and what I can do."

"And the Jews, sir?"

He took a slow, deep breath; his nostrils flared and his eyes darkened.

"The Jews are a peculiar lot. They practice their rituals, clinging to obsolete promises made by their prophets, which will never be fulfilled. They are a stubborn race, and unfortunately one that stands in the way of global oneness. As long as the Jews are here, staining the earth with their bloody, barbaric religion, the world can never fully come together. What you saw this morning was not merely a demonstration of my supreme authority and declaration of a new faith. It was also the sounding of the death knell for the Hebrews, once and for all.

"If they would abandon their old ways, I would accept them. But if not, so be it. You have seen what happens when we are not unified—wars, death, famine, disease, and the like. Therefore, there cannot be a single dissenting voice as we move forward. The Jews, they will run. They will scatter and they will hide, just as they have for centuries. But we will find them, and when we do," he said, his jaw tightly clenched, "we will *exterminate* them." He then relaxed his visage. "Do you have a problem with this?"

I couldn't think of one. Nor would I. "No, no sir. It is in your heart to do whatever you desire, and who am I to question the wisdom of your ways?"

Suddenly I became aware that the soldiers and Pietro had exited the temple proper. Beyond the walls I heard more rifle shots and screams. My face was drawn upward as I also saw lightning strikes descending from the sky, hitting specific spots all over the city.

Pietro was busy.

I turned back to see my president once again glaring at me.

"There is one more thing," he said. "For our economic strategy to succeed, there must be a universal identification system verifying a person's inclusion into our network. We have chosen to do this the simplest way possible. In order to know who is for us and who is against us, we have devised an identifiable mark that will be placed on every person. This mark will be a unique economic passport, enabling people to buy, sell, and trade anywhere in the world. Nothing like it has existed before, and the freedom and privileges which come with it make it irresistible."

Why is he telling me all this? Here? And now? I privately wondered.

"The reason I'm telling you this, Julien, is that because of Pietro's brilliant foresight, he began putting the infrastructure of this global network into production a year ago. Now, it's functionable and ready for implementation . . . *right now*. I would like to extend to you the high privilege of being the very first among billions to receive my mark. Do you accept this great honor I am bestowing upon you?"

"I would be a fool not to, sir."

He smiled, placing a hand on my shoulder and gently squeezing it.

"I knew you'd do it, Julien. You are a good man."

That moment represented a transition away from sit-down, formal interviews with him. From that point forward, all I really had to do was pay attention to what happened around me. I was afforded a front-row seat to history being made, and proximity to the one who was single-handedly making it. My spirit could hardly contain the elation. He was the One.

"I am *your* man," I said with adoration.

"I like hearing that. Now, our men will finish up here. Let's meet Pietro at the helicopter and head back to the airport. There's more work for us to do in Babylon, and besides," he remarked, gazing heavenward, "it looks like there could be a storm brewing."

CHAPTER
TEN

A WORLD ON FIRE

In an effort to make an example of the two slain Jewish prophets—and also, I suspect, to further mock and malign their religion—Pietro arranged to have their bodies put on display in Jerusalem for all the world to see. Their open coffins placed in the middle of the street sent a strong message to anyone else who dared oppose the One. The president's prophet also declared a seven-day holiday celebrating the demise of our enemies. A nonstop party erupted, as day and night, tens of thousands danced and drank themselves into delirium in observance of their deaths. The minister of affairs proclaimed it "Happy Dead Preacher's Day," and encouraged the exchanging of gifts in commemoration of it.

However, halfway into the week of jubilation, suddenly the two cold cadavers stood to their feet! And as their eyes opened, a shockwave of terror swept over the many thousands still in attendance, as well as millions of others as the event was being broadcast worldwide. And in full view of every eye, their bodies were lifted up into the clouds, disappearing out of sight. And with the terror of the moment still lingering, a great earthquake occurred in the city, destroying a portion of it along with killing seven thousand people.

But as strange as this phenomenon was, it only confirmed all the more the president's words to me three and a half years earlier: "De Clercq . . . it appears history has been awakened and we are entering an age of wonders." Once again he proved himself to be always one step ahead of what was about to happen.

In other news, I was surprised at how quickly the president's "Economic Loyalty Policy" went into effect. Pietro subsequently explained it to me further.

"I selected the use of epidermal stamp technology for the mark. Using indelible ink that penetrates the skin, we will apply it to every person participating in this program. The stamp will bear the president's profile image and his initials, much like the face of a coin. It will be administered for free on the right hand or the forehead at banks and religious centers worldwide. Without this mark, Julien, a person will be forbidden to transact business of any sort—from making a mortgage payment to buying a cup of coffee. We are happy to see you become the first to bear it."

This rapid success of the new mark system had, no doubt, been propelled forward by global announcements regarding the president's miraculous return from the dead. Video evidence of the assassination notwithstanding, there were skeptics who vocalized their doubts, claiming the attack was staged, using actors, props, and fake blood. But ultimately, the vast majority were converted to the truth, as eyewitness reports and phone footage of the assassination were released. This proved to be undeniable and conclusive documentation of the fatal nature of the president's wounds. Some of the videos contained graphic and gory images, and yet this did not deter the videos from becoming viral sensations, as billions viewed them.

An official medical report was also released online detailing the nature and extent of the president's traumatic head wound. It was signed by all five of the chief attending physicians and trauma-room surgeons present that Friday evening, effectively debunking conspiracy theorists. Other leading trauma surgeons and medical examiners also reviewed the official documents and photos, concluding unanimously that a cranial intrusion of this severity could not have been survived under any circumstance or subsequent emergency treatment. Added to the president's miraculous repertoire was the fact that within a day of his resurrection the horrible wound had all but disappeared from his head!

Further, following his assassination, the president visited some twenty nations, making personal appearances before crowds of more than 200,000 at a time. His now-famous Sunday morning palace press conference, along with video of Pietro's summoning of fire from the sky, only expanded his fame and legacy, further cementing his place in history.

As news of the Jerusalem temple incident spread, the president's office received an outpouring of enthusiastic support. A vast majority of countries and their citizens already resented the Jews, with their incessant claims to Middle Eastern real estate and the arrogant exclusivity of their religion. Anti-Semitism had been held in check because of the president's perceived affinity to Israel. But upon his self-coronation in the temple, pent-up resentment toward the Jews was unleashed. Public sentiment worldwide overwhelmingly backed the sacking of the temple and the elimination of the Israelis. "In a world finally becoming one," the president had repeated on his multinational tour, "there is no room for isolated nations, rogue races, or resistent religions."

I would add here that there was a most unusual follow-up to our temple visit that memorable Sunday. While leaving Jerusalem, the president remarked to his trusted confidant, "Pietro, the Jews believe their god's presence perpetually dwelt in that golden holy room. It would be a shame to leave it empty, now that I have replaced him. Perhaps we should ensure that it remains occupied. Why don't you arrange to have a likeness of me placed there permanently for all to see. Do what you have to do to display my glory in Jerusalem. And Pietro," he added, "make it interesting."

I heard him say these very words while we were being lifted above the bloody carnage at the Temple Mount. Subsequently, Pietro commissioned a likeness of the president to be carved out of the very same type of wood from which the ark of the covenant was made. This wood was used for the upper portion—torso, arms, and head—while the lower half—legs and feet—were fashioned out of Jerusalem stone taken from the Western Wall, a former place of prayer for the Jews. He then melted the gold that previously had covered the ark, using it for the statue's "skin." This gilded likeness proved remarkably true to the president's facial features. The iconic object stood an imposing 3.6 meters (12 feet) tall and weighed 861 kilograms (1,900 pounds). Add the height of the marble pedestal on which it stands, and it towers above the ground at just over 6 meters (20 feet).

The craftsmanship employed in this unique creation was meticulous, but that is not what made it so spectacular. Once completed, the herculean image was placed in the exact spot where the ark of the covenant once stood. Many thousands filled the former Jewish worship venue and the Temple Mount area for an official unveiling ceremony, which was also simulcast worldwide. At the sound of a trumpet, the minister of affairs pulled the sheet from the massive golden figure, prompting the entire audience to respond with awe and an extended ovation of praise. His creation exhibited all the pomp and glory of a Roman sculpture, standing with strength, perhaps also reminiscent of ancient Babylonian splendor.

And then something happened for which the world was not prepared, something Pietro had kept secret until that moment.

At the sound of Pietro Moretti's voice, the image was suddenly transformed, becoming humanlike. Its eyes became translucent, displaying color. Its golden skin seemed to glow with warmth. The chest of this magnificent beast expanded and contracted, as if breathing. Standing high above the mesmerized crowds, the image opened its mouth, and smoke poured out. Far from appearing mechanical or animatronic, the metamorphosis of this creature included malleable facial features, its expressions being fluid and lifelike. And out of its mouth came the very voice of the president. The intelligence and glory of the imposing figure both blanketed those gathered with terror and inspired their worship. They bowed before it as if it were the president himself.

Anyone found not bowing before this representative image was at once identified and executed in its presence. And the prescribed method of execution? When the image gives the order, the rebel is beheaded on the spot. The sight of bloodstains before the dreaded statue quickly became an effective deterrent to future would-be dissenters.

With unstoppable momentum already on his side, the president (who became popularly referred to as "the One") garnered even more strength through his Economic Loyalty Policy. From the time of its inaugural launch some three years ago, all individual trade, commerce, banking, online purchases, and digital transactions were suspended until citizens officially registered with the Economic Loyalty Policy Department (ELPD), overseen by the minister of affairs, of course. It really was a simple process.

First, individuals were required to register online, by mail, or in person. Then, they must visit the financial institution of their choice, where an approved epidermal stamp is administered by a licensed government official. The stamp effectively imprints a person with a "seal" utilizing the One's image. The process uses microneedles and an ink capsule containing biocompatible RFID (radio frequency identification) solution. Registrants can choose visible or invisible ink, but either way, it's permanent, and the process takes only a few minutes. This technology is detectable up to five feet away and contains rudimentary information tying participants to a global ELPD database. In other words, it verifies that they are officially registered to buy and sell, and that they are sworn devotees to the One. They are then free to pursue or maintain employment, access the internet for online purchases, sell merchandise (individually or as a business), buy food and gas, and so on.

The mark serves the people as their portal to financial freedom, an economic "ticket" providing access to the world of buying and selling. All who receive the mark are free to then use any method of payment they choose. It's a state-of-the-art symbol signifying total presidential allegiance, linking the heart to the pocketbook. In light of the alternatives—poverty and death—few refuse the mark. The overwhelming majority are convinced of its moral necessity and economic efficacy.

Even so, some, in arrogant defiance, stubbornly refused to comply with the economic edict. Like the Muslims and the Jews, the Christians also claim exclusivity concerning truth and God. Immediately following the mysterious vanishing of hundreds of millions almost seven years ago, little was heard from these radicals. But concurrent with that subsequent panic came a reborn awareness of the supernatural and metaphysical, expressing itself largely in a variety of religious pursuits.

Many would say this phenomenon of spirituality arose purely out of a fear of death, or perhaps a response to the worldwide devastation caused by the great disappearance. But a segment of this phobia manifested itself in a renewed interest in the story of Jesus Christ. Again, this wasn't abnormal, as multitudes across the globe were also seeking refuge in religion, philosophy, or self-actualization. What exacerbated the issue, though, was the Christians' disregard and contempt for others' beliefs. They were increasingly adamant about their convictions while simultaneously condemning opposing faiths and practices. This proved to be both unpalatable and unacceptable.

The crisis climaxed when the Christians were presented with the One's emblem, which they categorically rejected. In fact, so backward and brainwashed were they that *not one* of them registered to receive the beautiful mark. This, as you might imagine, presented a dilemma for the Christians. Their intolerance backfired on them, as they were forced to close businesses and were prevented from participating in financial transactions of any kind, except of course with other Christians.

In theory, this could have been allowed had they not continued their incessant preaching about judgment and treasonous rants about the One. Such vocal insubordination caused the president to become enraged, prompting him to authorize the arrest and execution of any and all such extremists. This further fueled public sentiment against those Christians, with local residents gladly informing authorities as to their whereabouts, largely underground domiciles and storage facilities. An official record was kept regarding how many of them were put to death. It's estimated to be significantly beyond 100,000.

However, this unfortunate distraction wasn't the worst obstacle hindering the One's agenda. Far more disturbing than a rogue religious sect on earth was what began happening to the planet itself.

Likely due to our failure to adequately address climate change, coupled with the unforeseen aftereffects of nuclear war, a series of catastrophic global disturbances occurred in the days following. According to climatologists, the aforementioned factors combined, triggering a "boomerang effect," impacting both the atmosphere and the subterranean makeup of our planet. Reverberations were felt deep into Earth's mantle, causing fissures at critical points below both land and sea. A gargantuan earthquake event occurred, producing a worldwide underground ripple effect, and prompting volcanoes, many dormant for centuries, to erupt. Molten lava spewed heavenward, literally showering the land with fire. These eruptions severely altered conditions in the troposphere and the stratosphere, with disastrous consequences. Giant, hundred-pound hailstones rained down upon billions. Fires burned up as much as a third of Earth's landmass. The smoke and heat generated made breathing difficult as winds carried the toxicity worldwide. The death toll and injuries were incalculable.

Then, a massive meteor event impacted the earth's oceans and seas, contaminating their water. The resulting tidal wave wiped out scores of trade ships and seaports. Another large meteor followed that one, violently penetrating earth's atmosphere, then breaking up and burning. The flaming debris fell into many major rivers, poisoning them. An unparalleled, lingering eclipse then occurred, darkening a large region of the planet.

Tragically, all this was but the beginning of our woes. Deep below the Egyptian sand, an enormous ground movement was detected. Shortly thereafter, a massive earthquake split open the desert, creating a crevice approximately one mile long and nearly 100 meters (328 feet) wide in places. The wider it became, the more desert it engulfed. So deep was the resulting chasm that underground gases ignited, sending ominous black smoke billowing up into the air.

And then an unbelievable thing happened, confounding scientists, zoologists, and evolutionists. Out of the black abyss appeared bizarre flying creatures—millions of them, by some estimates. To try to describe them seems almost futile, as their appearance was unlike anything ever seen by human eyes or conjured up by mortal imagination. I can only say that they looked like a freakish merger of man, horse, lion, and insect. Their faces were humanlike, and yet within their mouths were teeth resembling those of a lion. Their bodies were similar to locusts, though exponentially larger. A wing-span of some twelve to fifteen feet helped propel these grotesque beings through the air at accelerated speeds. Larger than a grown man, they were agile and skilled in their flight, having presumably dwelt for ages in immense caverns deep below. The final feature of these foul creatures was a scorpion-like tail, with a slight curve at the end.

The malevolent insect army flew in formation, as if under command by a superior leader. They would divide, traveling wherever there were people, be it to mainlands, inlands, or islands. And wherever they found us, they would instinctively attack, using their appearance to terrorize and their huge tails to torment. They effortlessly chased down individuals, knocking them to the ground. And with their giant wings hovering above, they would mount their victims, inserting their stingers into any available orifice or portion of flesh. It is universally reported that the curved tip of their stinger injects a toxin producing excruciating pain and a fiery, burning sensation that lasts for days. No one was safe from their pursuit. They could not be outrun, and they could not be defeated. They found ways into locked houses and buildings, breaking windows and bursting through barricaded doors. Some people managed to temporarily escape their wrath by retreating to cellars and storm shelters, but since the creatures appeared without warning, the overwhelming majority were caught unprepared and thus suffered horribly. This feared flying army was simply unstoppable.

Apart from administering heavy doses of painkillers, largely unavailable due to a prior shortage of pharmaceuticals, there was no relief for their excruciating venom. If obtained, most narcotics were used to attempt suicide, and yet curiously, no one succeeded in dying this way. The horde of mutant bugs blanketed us in terror for *five months*, then abruptly returned to their dark abyss beneath the Egyptian sand, where, as far as anyone knows, they remain to this day.

How these monstrous beasts could have evolved and survived for millions of years has the world's experts, and me, scratching our heads. Something obviously went horribly wrong in the evolutionary process, so much so that nature itself prevented these Frankenstein aberrations from joining the rest of the animal kingdom. Instead, they have remained imprisoned deep within the bowels of the earth, seemingly waiting for the day when man, through his selfish abuse of the planet, would accidentally release them. And that's when earth and nature, utilizing their most heinous creation, exacted their revenge.

The One remained in a state of seething fury during this period. It was the only time I ever saw him exhibit any degree of weakness, as even he and Pietro were powerless to halt the advance and menacing terror of these flying demons.

You would think nothing could compare to such a horrible plague, but you would be wrong. No one could have envisioned what happened next.

Another innumerable multitude of strange creatures simply materialized out of thin air.

Note: We are traversing in entirely new territory here. As if through the looking glass. Even now, I find it difficult to believe the world I am about to describe to you is my own. But I have now come to accept the unusual and the phenomenal to be ordinary. Ever since the One's return from death, the supernatural and the surreal have been normal . . . almost *expected*.

Again, I hesitate to even attempt a description of these beings to you, for I fear that, should earth survive, future generations who read this will find my characterizations far too incredulous. Nevertheless, my professional integrity compels me to tell the truth to the best of my ability.

As I mentioned, these additional foreign entities simply appeared, some say near or around the Euphrates River, and not far from Babylon, the Alliance capital. But this has not been verified. There has been speculation they may have come from outer space and are the long-awaited proof of alien life. If this is true, it once and for all answers the question of whether or not our space neighbors are friendly or hostile.

It's also entirely possible they arose out of the earth, much like their winged predecessors. However, there is no record of an earthquake in that region immediately before their arrival. So, the question of their origin remains a mystery, while the fact of their existence does not. Also undisputed is the nature of their agenda. But before I get to this, allow me to sketch in writing a composite description of these beings.

Fortunately, we live in an age where virtually every individual carries a high-definition video camera in his or her pocket. And captured footage of these creatures makes horror films of yesteryear pale in comparison. What we clearly see is that they are mounted upon animals resembling horses, yet with heads like ferocious lions. Out of their mouths proceed sulfuric fire and putrid-smelling, charcoal-colored smoke. Their tails are like elongated serpents, with heads bigger than a human hand. They coil, then strike with blazing speed and exceptional accuracy. The fanged bite from these scaly tails, along with the flame and smoke belching from their mouths, are their primary means of attack. And how do I portray the cavalry riding upon these horses? They are hideous beings, soldiers fitted with breastplates that I can only describe as demonic and maniacal. Their mere appearance would seize a beating heart with terror and anticipated torment.

I know what you're thinking. This truly *is* unbelievable. It has to be the subject of some grand delusion or mass hallucination. And I understand why anyone reading these words would be skeptical.

But believe it you must, for it actually happened exactly as I am describing it.

There was not an accurate method for numbering these murderous invaders, but conservative estimates from combined reports worldwide placed the figure at close to *200 million*! No city, village, or farm was immune from their attack. It seemed they intuitively knew where the people were. Amsterdam, Berlin, and Prague were hard hit, as were Krakow, Minsk, London, and Dublin. All told, one-third of earth's population was killed. One third. This number, when added to the dead from our previous nuclear wars and the great vanishing, put the total lost in the past seven years at around *four billion*, or well over half of earth's total population!

By this time, our planet had become a veritable wasteland of death, decay, and destruction. The stench of rotting corpses filled the air. Great cities had been reduced to uninhabitable wastelands, while decent men and women turned into beasts. The more calamity that struck, the angrier and more desperate we became. Some looked to the supernatural, even bowing in worship before the very creatures who tormented them, hoping perhaps to satiate their wrath. It did them no good. Others became violent, committing murder as food and financial resources grew scarcer.

Many citizens medicated, losing themselves in a mind-numbing haze of black-market opiates in an effort to escape from reality. Others immersed themselves in sexual pleasure as a way to counteract the mental anguish they were experiencing. And interestingly enough, there was even a resurgence of anger toward the Christian God. Even those who identified as atheists found themselves furious at the God of the Bible, and at Jesus Christ, whom they blamed for all these horrible plagues. Social media was saturated with vile, vitriolic rants against Christians and their deity, whom they charged with bringing these "judgments."

These calamities, and others, went on for months, as the entire planet maintained a vigilant state of emergency. The One assured us that, in time, all would be well and stability would be restored, but it did little to fend off the epidemic of fear that had enveloped earth. As for me, during this latest attack, I spent part of my time in a Babylonian bunker with others from the administration. Fortunately, I managed to dodge the awful suffering that had plagued so many others. My only discomfort, ironically, came as a result of the One's mark on my right hand, which I concluded had become infected. At random times, and for reasons unknown, it itched terribly, and I was afraid to scratch it for fear of damaging my skin or the emblem's face. However, after visiting one of our physicians, he could find no sign of infection, and sent me on my way. Still, on occasion I feel as if something is crawling beneath my skin, and no medicine, oral or topical, is able to relieve this prickly irritation.

For a short time after these incidents, we experienced what many referred to as the "eye of the storm," where we enjoyed relative calm. But this respite was but a brief hiatus, as more horrors were to come. Festering sores suddenly appeared on everyone who bore the One's mark. It was initially believed this was due to some form of postradiation poisoning, but it was ultimately diagnosed to be a side effect of the experimental ink used in the administration of the mark on the hand or forehead. A worldwide broadcast from Babylon assured the world that this discomfort would be temporary, and that a treatment would be forthcoming.

Apart from this internal issue, there were more, external problems with which to contend. The oceans' viability continued to deteriorate, and every fish and sea creature known to man died. This not only filled the waters with more blood but also produced an unimaginable, unbearable stench. Further, perhaps as a result of past nuclear detonations and the recurrent volcanic activity over the last several years, the earth's ozone layer became significantly depleted. This allowed a deadly amount of the sun's ultraviolet rays, along with intense heat, to penetrate the atmosphere, scorching the earth and its inhabitants.

It was as if the air itself were on fire. Polar ice caps began melting, in turn raising the oceans' water to historic levels, over 60 meters (200 feet). Coastal cities and regions were flooded, and the state of Florida disappeared completely underwater, as did most of America's coastlines. All these are now submerged under a putrid-smelling, bloody sea of death. Maritime transport is a relic of the past.

Lastly, the cosmos once again turned against us. Only this time, the light of day was removed. Time itself seemed to stand still, as a velvet curtain blanketed the earth. So dark was this period of night that it drove many to absolute madness.

My role in the midst of all this confusing, apocalyptic activity was, to put it bluntly, to try to keep my wits. A clear head and steady emotions were my salvation. That, and my trust in the One, who I was confident would triumphantly lead us out of this cosmic chaos.

As it turns out, he was occupied with doing just that.

CHAPTER ELEVEN

THE LAST
INTERVIEW

When I was originally hired for this job, I spent the first three and a half years working from home, periodically commuting to Rome and Babylon for my interviews. The morning I hurriedly took the train to Paris following the president's assassination, however, I never returned to my tiny Brussels apartment. The administration arranged to have my clothes and personal effects sent to me, and even assisted in helping me find someone to rent my apartment. And so, having not lived there for more than three years, a rare window of opportunity opened for me in my work schedule, so I decided to return and check on its status.

Well, there was one other reason.

I had received word from a mutual friend that the gentleman to whom I was subletting had been killed by the recent cavalry of alien beasts. So, I flew to Paris midafternoon, subsequently taking the same Thalys train back to Bruxelles Central Station. From there, I had only a short cab ride back to my former address.

Upon arrival, I slipped my key into the lock as I had hundreds of times before, and stepped inside, where at once a familiar sensation came over me. The smell of that diminutive domicile flooded my mind with memories of countless days and nights spent there. I recalled the morning I had dashed out the door and down the steps, hoping to hail a taxi, in response to the mysterious text from Pietro. Looking to the left, I saw the kitchen sink, and I remembered leaving the previous evening's dinner dishes there. And due, I suppose, to my renter's untimely death, he had returned the favor.

I began the task of sorting through his things, boxing them up for giveaway. There wasn't time to track down relatives, and besides, he didn't leave much behind. Mostly clothing. My former neighborhood had deteriorated considerably since I last left it. There was no shortage of abandoned cars, apartments, and houses. Graffiti decorated the walls of buildings. Many shops had been looted and gutted. New residents who saw me arrive treated me as an outsider, and why not? Neither of us recognized the other. Most of the apartments on my second floor were empty, their doors kicked in, windows smashed, and contents long gone. For some reason, mine had been fortunate.

The One, along with his minister of affairs, was making plans for an extended stay in Jerusalem, during which he was to announce the establishment of an administration satellite office there. Having come to know him rather well, I suspected he had more grandiose plans than this, and that another military operation was in formation. I was scheduled to join him in a little over a week, whereupon I expected to learn more. It was during those ten days here in Brussels that I took time to compose the narrative you have been reading. It serves to record my personal reflections regarding the most memorable moments of the last seven years, both pleasurable and unpleasant.

My writing has proved to be not only a cathartic exercise but also a truthful antithesis to some of the rumors that have circulated regarding the One and his administration. Unlike any other, I am privileged to have been given a unique camera angle on recent world history as it was made. Though just thirty-three years old, and with only a relatively brief career as a journalist, I have been privileged to see more in seven years than most do in a lifetime. For that, I will always be grateful for this opportunity.

The One's official memoir has yet to be written, as the story isn't over. My ongoing research concerning that task for which I was hired is stored on a separate hard drive in a secure location in Babylon. The volume of material I have gathered in these seven years will more than suffice for a substantive autobiographical account . . . when the time comes.

The morning after my return home to Brussels, I read that the Chinese army, along with other army nations from the East, had crossed over the Euphrates River and were heading north. The Euphrates, having previously been flooded due to massive ice melts in the Ararat Mountains, had mysteriously and suddenly dried up, enabling these armies to cross. By all indications, these armies, having been in general agreement with the administration as allies, were marching up toward Jerusalem. It was popularly assumed they were amassing in force to support the One's larger efforts in the Israeli capital and the surrounding region. It was an assumption I hoped would prove true.

But while the Alliance military effort was occupied with affairs in Jerusalem, something else unexpectedly occurred. Rogue nations from the north, led by regrouped Russian Federation armed forces, along with a patchwork military contingency made up of a small Islamic regime and a handful of republics of the old Soviet Union, swiftly moved south, launching a surprise attack on the capital city of Babylon. The city had been left largely unguarded, save for minimal armored artillery, as there had been no overt indications such an aggression would, or could, happen.

Fortunately, Pietro and the One were not in residence at the time of the attack. Regrettably, news footage shows the city itself, along with the administration complex and the presidential palace, leveled and in smoldering ruins. News of this shocking, uncharacteristic defeat enraged the world's rightful leader, and from Jerusalem he vowed vengeance against his new enemies. On a personal note, I hoped my files remained untouched in their secret underground location, along with other sensitive government documents. But in the event they, too, were compromised and destroyed, I had made encrypted backup copies.

Later that week, I received a secure email from the One's aide stating that he and Pietro were traveling somewhere south of Jerusalem to confront the Jewish resistance who had barricaded themselves in a canyon area there. The message indicated the president had not forgotten his promise for me to join him in Israel. "Don't worry," the note concluded. "You will hear from him shortly."

While waiting for his summons, I proactively packed my bag in the event I had to leave suddenly. With some leisure time to think, I continued chronicling my personal reflections on these last years. I contemplated how much the world had changed since the day I stood up at the president's inaugural press conference. As a planet, we had already been through excruciating turmoil with the sudden disappearance of hundreds of millions. And there were countless numbers who were never able to cope with both the loss and the mystery of this perplexing event. My own puzzlement wasn't as much personal as it was global. I personally wasn't close to any of those missing, and therefore avoided grief's knock at my door. Rather, my interest was more professional and philosophical.

At that time, I had written a short piece for the *Belgian Daily Press*, entitled "Where Have All the People Gone?" In it, I explained the various theories of those who conjectured about the disappearances. The two most popularly proposed hypotheses were that these millions were abducted by a superior alien life form, or were spirited away by "God." I suppose you could argue the two are the same, both being from somewhere "out there."

Conceivably, an advanced species would, or could, possess the technology either to instantly abduct humans without a trace or to vaporize them into thin air by means of some futuristic weapon. Regarding the God explanation, I was vaguely familiar with what is referred to as the "Rapture doctrine" embraced by some in the Christian church. This belief states that before God's wrath is poured out on earth as outlined in the biblical book of Revelation, Christians will be taken away to heaven, sparing them that judgment experience.

In my youth, the only Christians I knew were Roman Catholics, and they never talked about their faith, at least not to me. I supposed it could be argued, as many Christian believers have in recent years, that the awful calamities we have experienced actually are a form of judgment. For me, however, this was just another fear tactic used by institutional Christianity to frighten people into submission and servitude to the church. It's no different from similar historic strategies employed by Christendom, dating back to the Dark Ages and before. Threats of hell and eternal punishment have long been their *secret weapon* when attempting to persuade unbelievers to commit to their cause.

Further, this thread of logic requires not only the existence of God but the Bible's reliability, which has long since been disproved. Notwithstanding my innate skepticism of three and a half years ago, I do now believe in the divine, just not in the one described in the Jewish and Christian Scriptures. It simply doesn't stand to reason that their God exists. For if he does, where has he been the past seven years? Why hasn't he done something to help his creation? Why so inactive? So distant? So uncaring? For me, the silence from heaven is deafening, and a convincing polemic against his actuality.

I also find practical flaws in the Christian explanation, as it also denies the obvious *natural* causes of earth's woes these past seven years—such as rogue nations starting wars, multiple nuclear detonations, the environmental effects of earthquake-induced volcanic eruptions on the atmosphere, and the cumulative effects of global climate change. Those are observable, verifiable, scientific facts that cannot be denied.

"And, like most rational adults, I will cling to science over superstition every time," to quote myself. My article closes by restating the question, "So, where did all the people go?" I answered, "I don't know. And neither do you. A more important, and relevant, question is, 'What do we do now, and how can we move forward?'"

Little did I know at that time, but my answer, *the* Answer, came in the form of a great leader, the likes of which the world has never known. I do believe in him. I'm not sure, however, I can be absolutely certain of anything these days, including my own belief or skepticism. If the last seven years have taught me anything, it's that another supernatural surprise could be waiting just around the corner.

So here I now sit, in my old apartment. The flickering light bulb hanging above me reflects the spotty electricity in our area. Through my second-floor window I see burned-out automobiles, garbage in the streets, smashed windows, billowing smoke in the distance, and periodic shouts and screams amid sporadic gunfire (though personal firearms are still prohibited in Alliance nations). This is what we have done to ourselves. This is what happens when individuals, communities, states, and nations refuse to yield themselves to One who offers peace, safety, and prosperity. His genius and divinity manifested as an angel of light in the midst of history's darkest hour. And yet, some would still refuse to acknowledge him, even after his miraculous return from death and the healing of his fatal wound. Beyond a reasonable doubt, he proved himself a super-politician, a prince of peace, and the quintessential diplomat.

The whole earth marveled at him when he took office, but so much more so after his resurrection. He turned our confusion and chaos into hope and stability. He enabled us to put aside our differences and to come together under a common banner of humanity. And yet, those with rebellious religious persuasions persist in holding themselves aloof and apart from the rest of us just to perpetuate their foolishness.

For these people, their superstition is their own worst enemy. And that, I am convinced, is a primary reason we are suffering so severely. I am in agreement with what Pietro said to me in Jerusalem the day of the temple raid. "They deserve what is coming to them." I wish things could have been different, but each person must make his or her own choice.

As the One has said, "Get on the train, or get on the tracks."

But regardless of reasons, religions, and regrets, here we are. And here I am, waiting for the call or message signaling my final departure from Brussels.

Realizing I hadn't eaten since morning, and as I had grown weary of microwaveable dishes, I grabbed my jacket and left the apartment, walking three blocks to a local café I had frequented when I lived here. I was happy to see the tiny restaurant had some-how managed to survive, though upon my arrival there were no patrons.

"Julien? Julien De Clercq? Is that you?" a woman's voice called out from behind a serving window.

"Mevrouw Dumont!" I exclaimed. "How are you?"

The café owner looked much older than I remembered. Though it had only been a few years since I last saw her, the lines in her face told the story of a woman who had experienced considerable suffer-ing. I couldn't decide if she looked sixty-five or seventy-five. But it didn't matter. We embraced, and she gave me the customary triplet kisses on my cheeks.

"It's so good to see you. What have you been doing with your-self? I haven't seen you in the neighborhood in many years."

"I've been working abroad, writing . . ." I hesitated, stopping myself from divulging anything that would prompt more probing questions. No one outside a close circle of friends knew I had been selected for this prestigious job. And now certainly wasn't the time to divulge that information.

"Work is difficult to find," she said, waving her finger. "You are one of the lucky ones. After my Maarten passed away last year, I feared we may have to shut down. But we have been in this little place for more than thirty years. Thirty years! I ask you, Julien, how could I let it die? Look around. Not many have made it through the troubles. And yet, here I am. I cannot afford help, so I cook. I serve. I clean. I do everything. It's just me now."

It was refreshing to see a familiar face, and one so friendly. I sat at a table by the front entrance. My old friend brought a bottle of water and a well-worn menu.

"With deep apologies, we no longer have fish or meat dishes," she sheepishly explained. "Not since the oceans turned bad and the scarce meat became too much for me to pay for. We purify water with boiling. You understand, yes?"

"Of course I do. What do you recommend, Mrs. Dumont?"

"My special today is veggie pasta with garlic and sprouts, and Belgian *frites*." She announced the selection with great pride in her voice. But I suspected, considering food shortages, that this was likely the featured special *every* day.

"Sounds good. I'll have that."

She collected the menu and enthusiastically scurried off to the kitchen to begin preparation, a song on her lips. Apart from her excitement at seeing a recognizable face, I also suspected I had been her only customer this day.

I checked my phone. No word from Israel. Meanwhile, the

newswire reported that Asian troops, having crossed the now-passable Euphrates, were rapidly moving north and closer to Jerusalem. Whether the Israeli capital is their ultimate destination is unknown. Public information is notoriously unreliable these days. But one thing I had learned from watching the world from the safety of the One's inner circle was that there are no longer such things as "insignificant developments." Every action has set in motion another, producing rippling effects that impacted surrounding nations. I wondered as to the real agenda of this military deployment, and when rumors regarding other armies in similar stages of mobilization would be corroborated or proven false. In an age of uncertainty, hearsay is whispered through the wire, confusing and complicating the geopolitical world. And as always, threatening peace.

Peace. And safety. Phantom friends to our planet as of late. There is some degree of amazement when one thinks how we have even lasted this long. How many more creatures from beneath and bombardments from the sky can we endure? How many more diseases and plagues? Can the planet even hold itself together if another global earthquake event occurs? And what is there left for humankind to do to itself? With less than half the population from seven years ago, surely those who remain understand the absolute necessity for finding a way to coexist? Are there more hidden nuclear devices that will be rendered active for deployment? How many more have to die or be incinerated by war before we come to a mutual understanding of survival and relative harmony? These unanswered questions bounced around in my brain.

"Julien, my friend." Mrs. Dumont's voice from the kitchen broke my spell of concentration. "You are staring into the wall like a crazy man." She laughed nervously. "Too many lose their minds in these times. Don't be one of them, okay?"

"My apologies. I must have been daydreaming. It's been a long day, and my work—"

"You shouldn't work so hard," she scolded while making her way to my table, hot dishes in hand. "We need more love, not work. And I am hopeful the One will bring it to us soon."

Momentarily glancing out the window to the street, she lowered her voice, almost to a whisper. "I wonder if he will help us, if he even *can*," she remarked skeptically.

"Me? I have only heard what others have told me about him. I have never personally seen him, or his miracles. And yet look," she said, offering her stamped hand. "I am a 'loyal devotee,' and I pay him homage. Some believe he is divine, while others privately murmur that he is a devil. But me? I do not know. And who am I to say? Just an old woman who runs a dying café in Brussels. Nothing more."

She waited for my response, and when she could wait no longer, she spoke again in a voice revealing her French-German heritage. "So, what about you, Julien? What is your opinion of him? Who do you say that he is? God or devil?"

I was careful not to start a controversy with a woman holding hot dishes in her hand. But at the same time, I was not about to publicly deny the One I had come to know and trust. I was also careful not to reveal my privileged position and access to him.

"Like you, Mrs. Dumont, I have his image on my right hand. Officially, I, too, have sworn my allegiance to him. Privately? I can say this with honesty: I have friends who have met him, and even met *with* him. They tell me he is everything he claims to be. And the wonder of his reappearing, along with the miraculous works he has done, makes me a believer. I have no reason to doubt."

I paused to read her face, then attempted to interject a bit of levity into the conversation. "But who am I? Just a young writer . . . talking to a dear old friend. Nothing more."

"Hmmpf," she responded, seemingly unconvinced in her own mind. She placed the bowls before me and smiled. "Enjoy."

THE LAST INTERVIEW

Patiently standing tableside until I took my first bite, she awaited my approval, which I gave her with a nod, a smile, and an enthusiastic thumbs-up. The food was good, but not the caliber I remember from years past. Nevertheless, as I had not eaten all day, I devoured the dish's contents.

Daylight had turned to dusk in the brief time I had been there at the café. Mrs. Dumont came to collect the empty bowls, wiping her hands on her apron as she approached the table.

Anticipating that she was about to inform me she no longer served dessert, I preemptively asked for the bill. She grinned. "No, my old friend. There is no bill for you. My payment is seeing you again today. You have brought me good memories and more joy than money can provide." There were tears in her eyes.

I was so struck by her kindness, and attempted to pay her anyway. "Please," I countered. "Allow me to pay for my delicious meal." I held out my right hand, demonstrating my willingness to pay, but she insistently refused, pushing it away.

I stood, and we embraced once more. She reached out and took hold of my hands. The tears now escaped her eyes and rolled down her wrinkled cheeks.

"Julien, don't wait another three years to come see this old woman, okay? I may not be around that long," she said with quivering lips.

I gave her hands a squeeze. "I promise, Mrs. Dumont."

Before leaving, I covertly tucked a ten-euro note beneath my plate.

The weather, having long been unpredictable worldwide, was unusually cool on that April night in Brussels. I turned my collar up for the short walk back to my apartment. The streets were empty and dark.

For the next few days, I wrote and wrote. And waited. Ten days had passed since I last heard from the president's office, and I was

INTERVIEW WITH THE ANTICHRIST

beginning to worry, and to grow a bit impatient. After taking a spot
bath, due to water rationing, I fell back on my couch and opened
my laptop in hope of catching the latest news. No sooner had I
securely logged on than my phone began vibrating. The Caller ID
read, THE ONE.

"Hello, sir!"

"Julien, how are things in Brussels? How's the old apartment?"
he inquired. He seemed to always know where I was.

"I'm fine, sir. Just writing and—"

"Julien," he interrupted, "things are quite tight with my schedule at the moment. However, I did have a small block of time before
meeting with my military counsel this evening to call and let you
know what's about to transpire . . . for the *official record*."

"Of course," I replied. "A phone conversation is as good as
being in person."

"Of course it's not," he corrected. "But it's all we have right
now. So, let's have a quick interview, only instead of you asking the
questions, I will simply give you the answers and the information
you need."

His tone was sober and resolute. In the span of five seconds,
he had transitioned from a cordial greeting to a business meeting.
I, meanwhile, was frantically rummaging through my satchel for
pen and pad.

He began, "The next few days here are going to be historic. In
fact, I believe they will prove to be the defining moments of my
rule." There was a pause, and one so long and silent that I thought
we might have lost the connection. But then I heard his voice again.

"Julien, there's something we haven't talked about. Something
I have suspected for a long time but only recently confirmed. Do
you remember that day in the palace library when I described my
postmortem experience to you? What happened to me while I
was dead?"

166

"Yes, sir. I do. It's all documented. If you like, I can read—"

"Then you also remember I told you I heard a voice telling me I was not alone?"

"I *do* remember that," I replied.

"That wasn't the only time I heard the voice, Julien."

With those words, I could feel the hair on my arms and the back of neck begin to bristle.

"It was the very same voice I heard that day many years ago at the pyramid. However, following my reappearance from the after-life, the voice returned, and with increasing frequency—in fact, just moments following our conversation in the palace library. It was the voice that confirmed my plans to travel to Jerusalem later that morning. And in the days and months that followed, it became more than a mere *thought* popping inside my head. Those voice-thoughts became suggestions, which in turn birthed strong desires within. And I acted on those desires. All of them. In fact, in the past forty-two months, I have done nothing apart from what that voice has told me to do. And it's no longer just an utterance deep inside me. It's become part of my conscience. And the essence of my soul. The voice and I are now indistinguishable. It is *me* and I am *it*."

I will admit, at this point I was feeling very uncomfortable and somewhat confused. I felt as if he were treating me more as a personal confidant than a professional scribe. And I had no idea why he was telling me all this.

"Are you getting all this, De Clercq?"

"Every word, sir. Please continue."

I heard him exhale. "I sensed there was a definitive outside force or entity serving as the genesis of this experience. So, I sought to discover it through meditation and connecting with my innermost self. And what I found . . . is simply beyond description. Though it is I who reigns supreme on earth, this source is also what empowers Pietro. Combined, the three of us flawlessly function in a unifying triad of divinity—three distinct persons, yet with one essence. All I can tell you is that it . . . the voice . . . the real *one, he* is pure light, knowledge, and freedom. And he has imparted his essence to me, and made me what I am. He is the reason I rose again. The reason I have influence and power. The reason I can subdue all things. It is because of him that I have ascended the heights and rule in glory. He is the explanation for why the world worships me!"

I was feverishly scribbling as fast as my hand could write. *But who is this "he"?* I wondered.

"And Julien?"

"Yes?"

"He wants to do the same for *you* . . . through *me*."

I stopped writing. Looking up from my pad, I stared at the blank wall before me. I didn't know what to say or how to respond. What was he trying to say? What was he promising? Was he telling me he was going to make me like him? I was so confused.

"But here is where we encounter a grave obstacle."

"An obstacle, sir?"

"Yes. You see, as it turns out, we are not alone in this universe, De Clercq. There are others out there like me. Like the One who raised me. Alternative forces who exist in the supernatural realm. Called 'gods' by some, these seek to thwart our will, especially as it relates to mankind and the world. They even seek to personally destroy us. And as I have communed with the voice within me, and with Pietro, we have concluded that a galactic confrontation is in the making. It has become apparent that these opposing entities have a sympathetic ear toward the Hebrews. And I have a theory as to why. But no matter, I will capitalize on this affinity, and we will use the Jews as bait to draw one of them out to meet us on the battlefield."

I picked up my pen again and wrote down his words, underlining "battlefield." *So that's the real reason he's in Jerusalem*, I thought.

"Yes, that's why Pietro and I have come to Jerusalem, along with a historic coalition of military forces from around the world. We will entice the Jewish god to muster an army of his own and settle the issue of global sovereignty once and for all. And following this victory, you and I can talk more about your own rebirth toward eternal enlightenment.

"Now, I fully realize all that I have just said must sound unbelievable to you," he added, "but hopefully by this time tomorrow, you will know it's true."

"I trust you, sir."

I said those words to him, but I'm not so sure I believed them. I wasn't prepared for such lofty rhetoric, even from him.

"Julien, I am telling you all this ahead of time, so you can be prepared when you see it for yourself."

"Sir?"

"I'm sending a car for you. It should be there within the hour. You'll fly on a private jet to Israel, and then be driven the short distance to Jerusalem, arriving here around 3:00 a.m. Get some sleep on the flight here or at your hotel. I want you ready by 6:00 a.m. Jerusalem time. Tomorrow will be a day for the ages, and I want you fully alert and prepared. Our ground forces having already been assembled, you will fly via helicopter with Pietro and myself to the rendezvous point."

"And that being where, sir?"

"Bozrah. Look it up. I'll see you in the morning."

And with that, he hung up.

"Bozrah . . . Bozrah," I repeated out loud while map-searching it online. "*There* it is."

I thought, *Why, of all places, would thousands of Jews seek refuge in a desolate spot such as that?*

Perhaps answers would come in the morning. For now, I place my packed bag by the door, and wait. I have never witnessed a *real war* before. What would it be like? Was I prepared for this? And was I in any danger? How long would it last? Do the Jews have any defense forces at all? And will their supposed celestial ally show up to fight for them? More importantly for me, what is this "rebirth to enlightenment" the president referred to? I suppose I am a man with lots of questions. But that figures. After all, I am a journalist.

Anxiously awaiting the car to arrive, I spend these remaining minutes thinking about all that has happened over these past seven years. It occurs to me that I have composed quite a bit of material regarding my personal recollections over this period of time. I reasoned it might be a good idea to send this file to a trusted friend for safekeeping . . . just in case.

I glance down at the mark on my right hand and see his image staring back at me. I was the very first among billions to receive the coveted emblem. Of all people, he chose me. Tomorrow, it will mean even more, being by his side in his most glorious and triumphant moment. I wonder what other wonders await me.

While thinking about all these things, that annoying itching in my right hand suddenly returns.

And I hear a voice whisper my name.

MEET THE ANTICHRIST

THIRTY INTRIGUING BIBLICAL REVELATIONS ABOUT THE COMING MAN OF SIN

1. What does "Antichrist" mean?

Anti means "against" or "in place of." Therefore, Antichrist will be a false messiah, Satan's counterfeit Christ. A substitute savior. Jesus warned in Matthew 24:11 that many false Christs and false prophets will arise at the end of days. Specifically, the Antichrist will mimic Christ, using miraculous signs and wonders (Matthew 24:24; 2 Thessalonians 2:9). He will claim to be God (2 Thessalonians 2:4), and will seek to rule the world (Revelation 13:5–8). But he will also be *against* Christ in that he will try to prevent Christ's millennial reign by destroying the Jewish people (Revelation 12:12–17). If Satan can annihilate the Jews, then he can prevent them from repenting and calling upon their Messiah to come and rescue them. And theoretically, if Jesus doesn't return at His second coming, He cannot set up his millennial kingdom on the earth, and thus Satan will continue to reign through Antichrist.

2. Where will Antichrist come from?

Daniel 9:26, speaking of the last days, tells us "the people of the prince who is to come" would one day destroy Jerusalem and the Jewish temple. This prophecy is linked to Jesus' words to his disciples in Matthew 24:2 and Luke 19:43–44. Jesus' prophecy was fulfilled in AD 70 when the Roman general Titus destroyed Jerusalem, along with the temple, scattering the Jews for the next twenty centuries. We now know the "people" referred to in Daniel's prophecy were the Romans, and therefore the "prince who is to come" (Antichrist) is of Roman ancestry. This could mean he is Italian. However, it could also simply mean he can trace his lineage to Roman origins, or to any of the nations that were under Roman rule (from Britain south to North Africa, and from Spain east to Middle Eastern countries).

3. What will Antichrist's character be like?

It is difficult for us to wrap our minds around the concept of a man like Antichrist. The Bible calls him a "beast" (Revelation 11:7; 13:1, 14–15; 15:2; 16:13; 17:8). The Greek word used in the book of Revelation is *therion*, meaning a "wild or brutal animal." This term is used some thirty-six times in Revelation to describe this individual, indicating Antichrist will be a ruthless, ravenous individual. And the fact that he is energized by Satan himself further confirms this image. However, he has many other traits that will contribute to his rise to power and his pursuit of political world dominance. Scripture indicates that he will be sly and intelligent (Daniel 8:23); a master communicator and self-promoter

(Daniel 7:8, 11; 11:36; Revelation 13:5); a political genius (Daniel 9:27; Revelation 17:11–12); an economic strategist (Daniel 11:43; Revelation 13:16–17); a military demagogue (Daniel 11:40–44; Revelation 6:2; 13:2, 4); and a religious messiah (2 Thessalonians 2:4; Revelation 13:8, 12–15).

He will also be extremely charming and cunning, a deceptive liar, just like his father, the Devil (Daniel 9:27; 2 Thessalonians 2:4, 10–12; John 8:44). He will have no regard for any moral law or standard other than himself (Daniel 7:25; 11:36; 2 Thessalonians 2:7–8). He will be unimaginably arrogant and will eventually utter obscene blasphemies against the God of heaven (Daniel 7:8, 11, 25; 11:36–45; Matthew 24:15; 2 Thessalonians 2:4; Revelation 13:5).

4. Will Antichrist be a Gentile? A Jew? Or perhaps a Muslim?

There has been plenty of speculation concerning the racial and religious background of the coming false messiah. Some have argued that he will be a Jew, a belief tracing all the way back to the second century. A popular reason for this view is taken from the King James Version of Daniel 11:37, "Neither shall he regard the God of his fathers." This, they say, is contextual proof that the Antichrist is a Jew because he will reject the Jewish God of his forefathers. However, the Hebrew word here for God (*elohim*) is better translated "gods." The Septuagint (the earliest Greek translation of the Hebrew Old Testament) also translates *elohim* as "gods." Believing the Antichrist will definitively be a Jew stems from a weak understanding of this verse.

It is more likely he will be a Gentile who will have no regard for the religion or pagan gods his ancestors worshiped. Further, where Revelation 13:1 pictures this beast "coming up out of the *sea*" (emphasis added), John chose a word he used elsewhere in Revelation that refers primarily to Gentile nations (17:15). The coming world ruler will preside over the nations during what Jesus called "the times of the Gentiles" (Luke 21:24). Lastly, Antichrist will seek to destroy the Jewish people and commit blasphemy in the Jewish temple (Daniel 7:25; 9:27; 11:41, 45; 2 Thessalonians 2:4; Revelation 11:2; 12:6; 13:7). It is not likely a Jew would do such things.

But it has also been speculated that Antichrist could be a Muslim. In the Quran, the prophesied Muslim messiah is called the Mahdi, and possesses many of the characteristics of the Bible's Antichrist. He rides on a white horse, slaughters Jews, establishes his headquarters in Jerusalem, and reigns for at least seven years. In Islamic eschatology, however, there is quite a bit of confusion and contradictory information concerning the last days, making it difficult to put together any sort of sensible understanding of them. Also, the Muslim prophet Muhammad borrowed many of his ideas about the end times from conversations he had with Christians and Jews. Further, it is highly unlikely a true Muslim would ever sign a covenant protecting Israel and allowing them to rebuild their temple on a Muslim holy site. And lastly, it is unthinkable that a Muslim would ever claim to be God (Allah) and thus commit the greatest blasphemy possible according to Islam. He would be seen as the ultimate infidel among his fellow Muslims, whose great confession is, "There is no God but Allah."

Therefore, Antichrist will most likely be a Gentile.

5. Is there any chance Antichrist isn't a real person at all, but rather a governmental system? Or artificial intelligence? Or perhaps even a woman?

I see four ways to explain the concept of "Antichrist":

Possibility 1: He is a figment of John's imagination. Nothing more than the random ramblings of an aged, exiled Jew. You could attribute John's bizarre, apocalyptic Revelation tale to "post-traumatic stress from being plunged in boiling oil syndrome."[1] Of course, if this is true, nothing in Revelation can be taken seriously or ever be considered prophetically trustworthy or applicable to our lives.

Possibility 2: "Antichrist" is a symbol, pointing to something other than an individual—perhaps a governmental system, a secret committee of world leaders, or even artificial intelligence. Some see a broader interpretation of the term as simply referring to an evil end-times government marked by Antichrist-like characteristics. This view stems from a symbolic interpretive approach to the book of Revelation, and also because the Antichrist and his government are portrayed as inseparable.

Possibility 3: "Antichrist" is merely representative language, personifying the principle of evil itself. He is not actual, personal, or tangible, but rather abstract and metaphysical. Because 1 John 4:1–3 references the "*spirit* of the antichrist" (emphasis added) and because a literal interpretation of Revelation is rejected, this "spirit" must point to an evil *system*, not an actual person who is against the true Christ.

But if Antichrist is merely a concept pointing to the general principal of evil, then what do the rest of the characters and events found in Revelation represent? Are they also literary devices meant to illustrate additional spiritual truths? And with what authoritative deciphering tool do we accurately interpret their supposed symbolic meaning? This purely symbolic approach collapses under its own weight.

Possibility 4: Antichrist is a real person, and will appear in the end times exactly as the Bible describes. The word *antichrist* is used five times in the New Testament, and each time it refers to an *individual*, individuals, or the *spirit* of a specific individual (1 John 2:18 [2x]; 2:22; 4:3; 2 John 1:7). The "*spirit* of antichrist" is self-explanatory, meaning it doesn't exist by itself, but rather *comes from* Antichrist. This godless attitude/activity was active in John's day and is synonymous with the evil and lawlessness predicted in the end times (2 Thessalonians 2:7).

INTERVIEW WITH THE ANTICHRIST

How one arrives at a conclusion concerning the nature and reality of Antichrist is determined by the interpretive approach used. In other words, if the prophecies found in Daniel and Revelation are deemed "too bizarre and unbelievable to be taken literally," then it is John himself who must then be viewed with great suspicion. For who but a deranged old man dealing with the trauma and despair of exile would experience such hallucinogenic scenarios as depicted in the book of Revelation? And if this be the case, then how could we ever be confident concerning John's recollection of the life and times of Jesus Christ as recorded in his gospel? Or what about his other three epistles? Are they now suspect too?

And there goes one-fifth of the New Testament.

So, it is best to see the Antichrist described in Scripture as an actual person, not simply a system or a last-days government. And keep in mind, Satan is the evil entity behind both the *spirit* of the Antichrist and the man himself (2 Thessalonians 2:9; 1 John 4:3; Revelation 12:12–17). And speaking of this, Scripture repeatedly refers to Antichrist as a man, using male pronouns, and therefore negating any possibility he could be a woman (2 Thessalonians 2:3; Daniel 7:25; 11:36).

We see further scriptural depictions of Antichrist as a real person through the words of:

- Daniel (Daniel 7:8, 20, 24–25; 8:23, 25; 9:27; 11:21, 24, 31, 36–37)
- Zechariah (Zechariah 11:15–17)
- Paul (2 Thessalonians 2:3–4, 8–9)
- John (1 John 2:18–19, 22; 4:3; 2 John 1:7; Revelation 6–20)[2]
- Jesus (Matthew 24:15, 24)
- Angel (Revelation 17:7)

6. What are Antichrist's "names"?

Scripture assigns many names to this coming individual, including:

- the little "horn" (Daniel 7:8)
- the insolent "king" (Daniel 8:23)
- "the prince who is to come" (Daniel 9:26)
- "one who makes desolate" (Daniel 9:27)
- the "king" who does as he pleases (Daniel 11:36)
- the foolish, worthless "shepherd" (Zechariah 11:15–17)
- "the man of lawlessness" (2 Thessalonians 2:3)
- "the son of destruction" (2 Thessalonians 2:3)
- the "lawless one" (2 Thessalonians 2:8)
- the "antichrist" (1 John 2:18, 22; 4:3; 2 John 1:7)
- "the deceiver" (2 John 1:7)
- the rider on a white horse (Revelation 6:2)
- the "beast coming up out of the sea" (Revelation 13:1)

7. Is Antichrist a homosexual? What do we know about his sexual orientation?

Some believe the coming world leader will be a homosexual, an interpretation largely derived from Daniel 11:37, which says he will "show no regard . . . for the desire of women." And from a surface reading, this conclusion makes sense. For what could be more blatantly anti-God and contrary to both nature and Scripture than for a man to reject the biological and natural sexuality assigned to him by the Creator? Taken at face value, this appears to be a reasonable interpretation of this passage.

Upon further study, however, other interpretations arise. Some commentators understand the phrase "desire of women" not as referring to the natural desire of a man for a woman, but rather referring to the Messiah himself. Traditionally, Jewish women in Old Testament times desired to be the mother of the promised

Messiah (Genesis 3:15). And the King James rendition of Haggai 2:7 calls the Messiah "the desire of all nations." In other words, the Messiah is the desire of all nations, and since the coming Antichrist will have no regard for this "desire of [Jewish] women," it simply means he has no regard for the real Messiah.

However, we find another understanding if we simply keep reading in Daniel 11. In verses 37–39 we find a more appropriate contextual answer: "Nor will he show regard for any other god; for he will magnify himself above them all. But instead he will honor a god of fortresses . . . He will take action against the strongest of fortresses."

It is more likely what Daniel was referring to here was that Antichrist's passion for power will so completely dominate him that he will have no time or desire for a normal relationship with a woman. This doesn't necessarily mean he is a homosexual. It simply means his mistress is military might and power. He is consumed more by them than by lust or love.

8. Are there any prophecies currently preparing the way for Antichrist's appearing?

Unquestionably, yes. First, Scripture shows that the Antichrist cannot appear unless the nation of Israel exists and is currently living in the promised land. This has already happened, as Israel officially became a nation again on May 14, 1948. Since that time millions of Jews have moved from around the world, flooding back home to Israel. This is an ongoing fulfillment of a prophecy given by Ezekiel some 2,600 years ago. In fact, the Jewish nation *must* be reborn and living in their homeland for the events of Revelation to unfold (Jeremiah 30:1–5; Ezekiel 34:1–24, 37; Zechariah 10:6–10). Today, more Jews are living in Israel than at any time in the last twenty centuries.

Second, the Bible says that the Antichrist will be revealed around the time of great apostasy in the last days (2 Thessalonians

2:2–3; 1 Timothy 4:1–3; 2 Timothy 3:1–9, 13; Jude vv. 17–19). This apostasy constitutes a falling away from the faith, which we are witnessing in our current age, both in formerly Christianized nations (America and England) and in the church itself. A falling away from the faith is one of the precursors that will prepare the world to accept the Antichrist when he appears on the scene. He will step onto the global stage only after humanity has purged itself of biblical truth.

Third, through the Temple Institute, the Jewish faithful have already drawn up plans for the third temple to be erected on the Temple Mount. They are training priests, constructing altars, sewing priestly garments together, and even sacrificing animals. All they need to make this dream a reality is for some sort of peace treaty to be signed giving them access and permission to begin construction on the Temple Mount. I believe this will happen when the Antichrist rises to power following the Rapture. Prophecy makes it clear this will happen, after which the "abomination of desolation" will be set up when Antichrist enters the temple, proclaiming himself to be God (Daniel 9:26–27; 11:31; 12:11; Matthew 24:15; 2 Thessalonians 2:3–5; Revelation 11:1–2; 13:11–13).

Some say this abomination of desolation already appeared in 167 BC, when Antiochus Epiphanes invaded Jerusalem and set up an altar of Zeus in the Jewish temple. He also forbade the Jews from practicing their religion, slaughtered a pig on the altar, and ordered sacrifices to be made to his god Zeus. However, we know this is not the ultimate fulfillment of Daniel's prophecy because Jesus himself, speaking some two hundred years after Antiochus's temple raid, predicted the abomination would take place at a future time (Matthew 24:15–22). So, the current, ongoing efforts in Jerusalem to prepare for the temple's construction is another "prophecy in formation" we can see happening before our eyes. This is a strong indication we are living in the era of Antichrist.

Globalism, or the movement for the world to unite and become one, is another developing movement paving the way for Antichrist. Nationalism is dying worldwide, and various efforts to unite the nations are gaining traction. Further, many countries are presently teetering on the edge of financial collapse, with many already falling into an economic abyss. This only makes international interdependence between nations more expedient, thus creating a need for a worldwide political figure to bring nations together. This is one of the factors that will enable a revived Roman Empire to emerge and unite countries following the catastrophe and chaos gripping the world following the Rapture. Universal oneness also ties in seamlessly with Satan's centuries-long desire to bring a united world under his control, beginning all the way back with Nimrod in Genesis 10–11.

One other global reality would be the fact that, for decades, world leaders have sought to bring peace to the Middle East. Right now, Israel and its surrounding neighbors continue simmering on the brink of war. The Middle East is a volatile powder keg that could explode into world war at any moment. All it takes is the firing of one strategic missile strike to ignite World War III. Because of this, the Middle East is ripe for peace, and the Bible says someone is going to bring that peace, albeit temporarily. He is called *Antichrist*.

9. What is the context of Antichrist's reign?

Scripture tells us the signing of Antichrist's peace treaty with Israel, not the Rapture, is what officially inaugurates the seven-year period upon the earth known as the Tribulation (Daniel 7:25; 9:27; 12:7; Revelation 12:6; 13:5). These seven years will be marked by a successive series of divine judgments upon a rebellious planet. These are called the seal, trumpet, and bowl judgments, and they culminate with the second coming of Jesus Christ, who brings wrath upon his enemies at this time (Revelation 6–19). This seven-year period will be the most terrible time in human history. The first three and a half years will see Antichrist ascending to power and primarily leading the world through peace and unity. During the last three and a half years, he will undergo a transformation in which he demands global worship.

Scripture also describes this time as "Daniel's seventieth week" (Daniel 9:25–27).[3] The latter half is called the time of "Jacob's trouble," or distress, because the Jews will suffer horribly during the final forty-two months (Revelation 12:12–17).

Again, what marks the beginning of this seventieth week (final seven years) is the signing of a covenant between the Antichrist and Israel. This is the next Tribulation-related prophecy on God's calendar.

I believe what precedes Antichrist's rise to international prominence are not only the prophecies and global trends we currently see in formation but also the Rapture of the church (John 14:1–3; 1 Corinthians 15:50–58; 1 Thessalonians 4:13–18).[4] When it occurs, this single event will trigger an avalanche of catastrophe, chaos, and panic worldwide. Fear will grip our planet. And into this crisis will step history's opportunist, Satan's man of the hour, who will bring calm to the storm. His political platform will be simple—peace and safety for all (Daniel 8:25; 1 Thessalonians 5:1–3; Revelation 6:2).

10. Have there been other Antichrist-like figures in the past?

Ever since his rebellion in heaven, where he aspired to "become like the Most High," Satan has wanted to be God (Isaiah 14:12–14; Ezekiel 28:11–19). This desire for deity has not only marked his own personal ambition but has also been displayed through his servants as well. We see it through the ruler Nimrod, who built ancient Babylon and the Tower of Babel (Genesis 10–11). We see it in other infamous world rulers who would not only follow a similar path to world dominion but also be great persecutors of the

Jewish people. Pharaoh and Nebuchadnezzar would be examples of this, and, as previously mentioned, Antiochus Epiphanes, who foreshadowed some of the same actions of the future Antichrist against the Jews and their temple. Other examples would be the Roman Caesars; the Roman general Titus, who destroyed the temple in AD 70; and Adolf Hitler. But all of these wicked men pale in comparison to the evil character and deeds of the coming Antichrist.

11. What does Antichrist's government look like?

The Bible describes the beast's empire in Daniel 2:31–45 (ten toes); and in Daniel 7:19–28 and Revelation 13:1–9 (ten horns). Satan's man will lead a ten-nation alliance, or confederation of nations, perhaps somewhat similar to the current European Union, only much stronger. This group of nations will effectively be a "revived Roman Empire." But how do we arrive at this conclusion?

First, Daniel describes four empires, and we know from history the fourth empire Daniel described was Rome (7:7–8), with the other three being Babylon (7:1–4), Medo-Persia (7:5), and Greece (7:6). However, a final form of the Roman Empire is portrayed as having "ten horns," later explained in Daniel 7:24 as being "ten kings" (or ten united nations). However, the problem is that the Roman Empire never existed in this ten-king formation. Therefore, this aspect of the Roman kingdom must still be future (i.e., in the Tribulation, Revelation 12:3; 13:1; 17:3, 12–13). Second, this revived Roman Empire is spoken of as being suddenly "crushed" by the "stone" of Messiah's future kingdom (Daniel 2:34–35, 44). This has also not yet occurred, as the ancient Roman Empire declined over time due to a combination of political, moral, and military factors. None of these relate to the establishment of Messiah's reign on earth. So, this remains an unfulfilled prophecy concerning a yet-future kingdom. Finally, if Daniel's prophecies regarding the previous four global empires were fulfilled literally, then why should we not expect the final prophecy concerning Antichrist's revived Roman Empire to also be literally fulfilled?

12. Will Antichrist's headquarters be in Rome or in Babylon?

We know from Revelation 6, 13, and 17–18 that Antichrist's kingdom has three components: political, economic, and religious. Revelation then devotes two entire chapters to Babylon, the capital of his empire (Revelation 17:15, 18; 18:1–24). The question is, what is "Babylon"—symbolically and actually? In Revelation, Babylon is a very important city, more critical to the end-time narratives than any other city with the exception of Jerusalem. Babylon is also the personification of the Tribulation-era evil government. She is pictured as a harlot, or prostitute, riding on the beast (Antichrist) in Revelation 17:3–5, 7. This city is also the center for an apostate world religion (Revelation 17:4–5; 18:1–2). She is also a global economic hub (Revelation 18:9–19). Babylon is responsible for killing many believers in Christ (Revelation 17:6; 18:20–21, 24). Ultimately, it will be utterly destroyed, never to be rebuilt again, due to her unrepentant immoralities, greed, and persecution of the saints (Revelation 18:8–10, 21–24). So, these are the things she represents.

But is "Babylon" really Babylon? Some see this as symbolic of Rome, based on 1 Peter 5:13 and also Revelation 17:9, which relates seven kingdoms to seven hills or mountains. Rome is a city built on seven hills; therefore, it is assumed that the empire's capital city, called "Babylon," must actually be referring to Rome. However, the text itself gives us a better interpretation. The seven mountains are explained as seven heads, or kings, which represent seven *kingdoms*. Five "have fallen" (v. 10) and are in the past at the time of John's writing (Egypt, Babylon, Assyria, Medo-Persia, and Greece), one "is" in the present at the time of John's writing (Rome, v. 10). And "the other has not yet come" (Antichrist's revived Roman Empire, v. 10). When the apostle John refers to a location as being symbolic, he typically tells us, as in Revelation 11:8, where Jerusalem is "*mystically* called Sodom and Egypt." So, without any other reason to interpret Babylon as anything else, we must assume that it is actual Babylon.

Six separate times in Revelation the city of Babylon refers to Antichrist's capital city (14:8; 16:19; 17:5; 18:2, 10, 21). We know from the Old Testament that Babylon is where mankind established a rebellion against God (Genesis 11:1–11). In fact, historically this city has long been an enemy of God and his people. Babylon is mentioned about three hundred times in Scripture, and every single time (with the exception of maybe one), it refers to the physical city Babylon. Also, 44 of the 404 verses in Revelation speak of Babylon (11 percent).

There are many practical reasons why Antichrist would want to rebuild ancient Babylon and establish his headquarters there. The area is rich with oil reserves and sits in a strategic geographical location between continents. Ancient Babylon is also located on the banks of the Euphrates River, a river twice mentioned in Revelation for demonic activity and as playing a key role for the armies of the East marching to Armageddon (Revelation 9:14; 16:12).

While one cannot be dogmatic, it would appear that during the Tribulation, the ancient city of Babylon will either be rebuilt or added onto and modernized to accommodate Antichrist's headquarters for his economic, political, and religious agendas.[5]

13. Will Antichrist control the United States during the Tribulation?

In the aftermath of the Rapture, the United States of America will most likely be decimated—economically, militarily, socially, and morally.[6] For this reason, I believe she will cease to be the world's superpower she once was. The United States will probably become dependent upon foreign aid and other nations. This could be a viable reason for her to be absorbed into, or partner with, other countries for inclusion into Antichrist's ten-nation coalition. There is also the probability of America being additionally weakened following the Rapture as a result of nuclear strikes, electromagnetic pulse attack, Islamic terrorist attacks, or simply due to the combined results of her moral, political, economic, and military implosion.

14. Will the Antichrist know he is the Antichrist? When does he find out?

The Bible does not tell us how or if the Antichrist fully understands his identity and connection with Satan. And it is unlikely he would be fully cognizant of this future role *before* the midpoint of the Tribulation. Here's why: There appears to be a turning point in Revelation 12, a midpoint hinge on which the Tribulation swings. Scripture indicates here that Satan attempts yet another coup in heaven and, along with his demons, is forcibly cast out of there and down to earth by the archangel Michael. At this midpoint moment in the seven-year period, something dramatic occurs.

The Bible says the Devil then realizes he now only has a short time left. Because of this, he goes on a rampage, igniting great wrath as he begins persecuting the Jews. This is a specific point in time when the Antichrist enters the temple, declaring himself to be God. Obviously, if he believes himself to be God, then he has become satanically possessed to a degree he has never known before. Though perhaps subconsciously motivated by demonic and satanic influence during the first three and a half years of the Tribulation, he now becomes a man enraged, fully under the control of the Devil himself.

15. Will Antichrist have a supernatural birth?

Some have speculated that Satan will attempt to mimic the birth of Jesus with the birth of the Antichrist. Genesis 3:15 is often cited, where the seed of the woman, which we know is prophetically referring to Christ, is pitted against the seed of the serpent, whom it is assumed is the son of Satan. But this sort of conjecture is more movie fiction than scriptural reality (ex.: *Rosemary's Baby*, *The Omen*, etc.). And there are at least two problems with this view.

First, there is no biblical indication that Satan possesses the power to impregnate a woman with his seed, producing a parody of the virgin birth. An argument *could* be made from an interpretation of Genesis 6:1–2, where the "sons of God" (fallen angels) took on human form in order to engage in sexual intercourse with mortal women. But again, Scripture is silent concerning Satan duplicating this heinous act. And it is believed those demons were locked away in chains following this perversion (2 Peter 2:4; Jude vv. 6–7).

Second, for Satan to produce the Antichrist in this way, he would have to know God's precise timetable for the Rapture and Tribulation so he could be born at just the right time. For example, he would have to be of a certain age (and thus born at a prearranged time) in order to be of age and politically positioned well enough to seize power following the Rapture. It is more likely the man who eventually becomes Antichrist will grow up as an "ordinary" person, and at some point open himself up to satanic influence.

Third, Satan does not need a miraculous birth to accomplish his agenda through a man who will be possessed by him. What is clear is that the Antichrist is empowered by Satan with all power and signs and false wonders (2 Thessalonians 2:9), and that he acts on the authority of Satan himself (Revelation 13:4).

16. What is Antichrist's primary agenda?

Among his objectives will be to gain a political platform that will lead to global influence. But his ambition goes even deeper than this. Antichrist will be the human vessel through which the Devil finally realizes his blasphemous and long-sought wicked desires. Part of Satan's appetite is to kill Christians, as he understands how important they are to God. However, Antichrist will also hate the Jews and Israel, because he knows God's plan is for the Jewish Messiah to return and save his covenant people. Following this, Christ will establish his 1,000-year kingdom upon the earth. And if this happens, Satan will be prevented from having the world for himself. So, if the Antichrist can kill all the Jews, there won't be anyone for the Messiah to come and rescue. Satan also hates the Jews because through that chosen race came the Savior, Jesus Christ, who defeated death and the Devil at his first coming.

Since the inception of his rebellion, Satan has wanted to be worshiped. He wants what God has. He wants the world. He wants people's adoration. He wants to *be* God. And like the one who empowers him, Antichrist has a heart baptized in sin, inflamed with self-love, and engorged with an insatiable desire to *be God*. Because Satan will possess the Antichrist, the Devil will vicariously live out his own dream through the man of sin.

And so, the rebellion that began in heaven long ago will culminate with the arrival and reign of the "willful king" (see Daniel 11:38).

17. Will Antichrist possess supernatural powers?

The Bible tells us that supernatural signs will accompany Antichrist's activity (2 Thessalonians 2:9; Revelation 13:11–16). Whether he will perform all of the signs and wonders himself is not known. Nevertheless, his arrival and administration will be accompanied by many convincing miracles, some or all being performed by the false prophet. An age of miracles will once again be inaugurated, not only through Antichrist's wonders, but also through the miracles performed by God's two witnesses (Revelation 11:3–6), as well as through the supernatural seal, trumpet, and bowl judgments administered by God himself on Earth and its inhabitants (Revelation 6–19).

18. Will Antichrist actually be possessed by Satan?

Yes. He will be the most satanically possessed man in history. When we piece together all of what Scripture says about this man, we conclude he is "Satan wrapped in human skin," speaking words and performing acts only the Devil would conceive of. In fact, other than when the Devil "entered into" Judas Iscariot to betray Jesus (Luke 22:3; John 13:21, 27), not a single other individual is said to have been actually indwelt by Satan. The Antichrist will be energized by evil, deputized by the Devil, and saturated in satanic pride (see Ezekiel 28:2, 9–12; Daniel 8:25; Revelation 13:4). He will be possessed—body, mind, and soul—by the demon Prince of Darkness. Again, his full possession most likely occurs at the midpoint of the seven-year tribulation.

19. How will Antichrist deceive the nations?

Antichrist's deception of the world will happen because of several reasons: First, as a result of the Rapture, people will be desperate and panic-stricken, more so than at any time in history. Hysteria and madness will be pandemic. Like a starving person eating almost anything put before him, these desperate people will be hungry for answers, safety, and hope. Part of Antichrist's agenda will be to provide these things to them, making promises he ultimately cannot keep.

Also, the Bible tells us his persuasive promises will be authenticated by satanic signs and false wonders (Matthew 24:24; 2 Thessalonians 2:9). Satan is a master counterfeiter, possessing the ability to do things that are virtually indistinguishable from actual miracles. He may even have the ability to perform real supernatural deeds during this unique period of history. Scripture uses the same words to describe these satanic signs and wonders as it does to describe those done by Jesus.[7] And in the context of the times, people will *want* to believe.

Third, Scripture says that because those left behind at the Rapture previously refused to believe the truth of God and the gospel, the Lord himself will send a deluding influence on them so that they might believe what is false (2 Thessalonians 2:10–12). This is one of the damning consequences of rejecting the gospel, and is a part of the abandonment wrath we see in Romans 1:18–32.

20. Can Antichrist do anything he wants? Does he possess unlimited power?

The man of sin will have great power unlike any person has ever possessed. Nevertheless, his power will not be absolute or unlimited. Aside from the previously mentioned miracles and wonders, he is bound by the parameters of Satan's inherent limitations as a created being. There is no indication he will be able to read people's minds, for example.

Some of Antichrist's satanic influence will result in him speaking unbelievably blasphemous words and being authorized to pursue his wicked, worldwide agenda (Revelation 13:5), persecuting and killing those who come to Christ during the Tribulation and exercising authority over all the earth (13:7). And yet, even with all these powers, he is still under the sovereign control of God. In each of the above verses we see the phrase "was given to him," meaning the Antichrist can do nothing outside of the boundaries God has set. The Father is the one in control of history, and he alone determines the boundaries and powers of his enemies (1 Chronicles 29:11–12; Job 42:2; Psalm 115:3; 135:6; Proverbs 16:4; Isaiah 14:27).

21. Who is Antichrist's right-hand man?

Revelation tells us of "another beast" who accompanies the Antichrist in his political power and popularity (Revelation 13:11–18). This man's primary role is to support and promote Antichrist and his evil agenda. He is called the "false prophet" (Revelation 16:13; 19:20;

20:10), and he is given the ability to perform miraculous deeds and wonders. He is the public relations man for Antichrist, promoting him much as the Holy Spirit promotes Jesus. His origin is a mystery, and though it is possible he *could* be Jewish, it is unlikely due to the nature of his actions against the Jews. He too is persuasive, with an appearance like a lamb but a voice like a dragon (Revelation 13:11). He is the one who is in charge of the religious aspects of Antichrist's empire. The false prophet also draws his authority directly from Satan (Revelation 13:12).

Among his abilities is bringing down fire from heaven, perhaps mimicking God's two witnesses in the latter half of the Tribulation (Revelation 11:4–6; 13:13–14). He is the one who ensures that an image is created of the Antichrist and placed in the temple (Revelation 13:14). He supernaturally causes the image to breathe and speak (13:15). And part of his duties involves enforcing Antichrist's economic program, not only implementing the mark of the beast, but also killing anyone who refuses to worship the image and the beast himself (13:15).

22. What is the "abomination of desolation"?

In Matthew 24:15–16, Jesus said, "When you see the ABOMINATION OF DESOLATION which was spoken of through Daniel the prophet, standing in the holy place . . . then those who are in Judea must flee to the mountains." Christ is referencing Daniel 9:27 and 12:11. In these passages Daniel predicts that the Antichrist will make a firm covenant or agreement with the Jewish people for three and a half years. That covenant will allow them to rebuild their temple, thus reinstituting the Old Testament sacrificial system. Specifically, the abomination here refers to the moment when Antichrist enters the rebuilt temple and proclaims himself to be God. At that time, Daniel tells us he will put a stop to sacrifices and grain offerings.

As previously stated, this end-times abomination was foreshadowed in 167 BC when King Antiochus IV (Antiochus Epiphanes) sacked Jerusalem, plundering the temple. At that time, he made the sacrifice of an unclean pig on the altar while also erecting a statue of Zeus in the Holy of Holies. So arrogant was Antiochus that he even put his own face on the statue, which he no doubt saw as appropriate since his name means "God manifest." During the intertestamental period, the Jewish Maccabean revolt retook the temple and cleansed it of this sacrilege.

Paul, in his prophecy, tells us Antichrist will also take his seat in the temple of God, "displaying himself as God" (2 Thessalonians 2:3–4). This abomination will continue when the false prophet sets up an image of the beast in the Jerusalem temple so the world can come and worship him there. And this abomination will continue for three and a half years until the return of Jesus.

Since Jesus, Paul, and John all speak of a *future* temple and Antichrist's abomination there, Daniel's previous prophecy concerning the same event could not have been completely fulfilled in 167 BC. Therefore, this prophecy must await a future fulfillment. The last temple was destroyed in AD 70, and a third temple must be built during the first half of the Tribulation in order for the prophecy to be completed. And when this abomination does occur, Jesus says, "run" for your lives (Matthew 24:15–21).

23. What is the "mark of the beast"?

In Revelation 13, John tells us the false prophet will cause the whole world to be given a mark on their right hand or on their forehead, and that without this mark no one can buy or sell. There's been endless speculation as to what this "mark of the beast" will be, but there are several things of which we can be sure.

First, only those who are destined for hell will receive the mark. Not one person who receives this mark will later confess Christ and become a Christian (Revelation 14:9–10; 16:2). This is a visible, tangible mark symbolizing that their fate has been sealed.

Second, not one believer in Jesus will take the mark (Revelation 20:4). Therefore, any person during the Tribulation who claims to be a Christian and then later takes the mark of the beast proves himself or herself to not truly be saved.

Third, as with many other satanic strategies, this mark is meant to duplicate and/or mimic something about Jesus—in this case his mark on the 144,000. Revelation 14:1 tells us the name of Jesus and the Father's name are written on the foreheads of the 144,000 Jewish male evangelists who are chosen to preach the gospel during the Tribulation. This (invisible) mark on them is a sign they are sealed and protected by God (Revelation 7:4).

So, what exactly is this "mark"? What will it look like? And what does the infamous "666" mean (see Revelation 13:18)? It is important to understand that every person who takes the mark will do it voluntarily, though the alternative is starvation and death. Most will no doubt take it for the sake of expediency or out of fear. The *purpose* of the mark is twofold: (1) to identify those approved and authorized to buy and sell by Antichrist's administration. Without the mark you will not be able to make a mortgage payment, buy online, or even purchase a soft drink. It will enable a person to participate in commerce. This mark will be administered beginning with the second half of the Tribulation, or the final three and a half years. It likely will *not* be some sort of microchip or epidermal implant. We know this because Revelation 13:16 makes it clear that the mark will be administered on (Greek *epi* = upon) the right hand or *on* the forehead, not *in* them.

The Greek word for "mark" John used here is *charagma*, an ancient word referring to the names or images of Roman emperors on Roman coins. Some slaves and soldiers under Roman rule also bore an identifying mark, symbol, or brand linking them to their master or their military allegiance. So, it is conceivable that this mark could depict the name or face (perhaps the profile) of Antichrist.

Further, nowhere does the Bible say this mark contains encoded information, such as bank account information or personal data. All it says is that the mark *enables* a person to buy or sell. So, for example, like your membership card at a shopping club (such as Sam's), which gets you through the door, the mark serves as your "membership card" or "commerce passport."

The existence of this mark of the beast does not necessarily cancel out the use of cash or credit cards. There may also conceivably be some sort of database that will identify who has and has not taken the mark.

(2) The second purpose of the mark is to identify the bearer as a worshiper of the Antichrist. Everyone who receives the mark will most likely see Antichrist as their "economic savior," provider of peace and safety, and protector from harm. They will also see him as divine, since he overcomes death and the grave.

We do not yet know whether this mark will involve some high-tech process, such as a visible epidermal tattoo utilizing some sort of detectible ink (such as a biocompatible RFID, or radio frequency identification) solution. Depending on the nature of the mark and the method by which it is verified for transactions, it may or may not be detectable by equipment. It could also be something as primitive as a brand.

Concerning the number 666, much has been written and speculated about it. The most often used decoding mechanism for attempting to figure out the meaning of "666" is *gematria*, a method of converting letters to their Hebrew alphabet equivalent and assigning a numerical value to them. This method has been used to try to link Antichrist to everyone from John Kennedy to Barack Obama. I do not believe anyone can currently decipher the identity of the Antichrist this side of the Tribulation by using this method. And quite honestly, any attempt to do so combines a large measure of both ignorance and arrogance.

However, John does say in Revelation 13:17–18 that those living during this time (Tribulation) who possess understanding will be able to calculate the number of the beast to be 666. Some have suggested that since the number seven is the number of perfection in Scripture, representing God, six then represents the number of man since he was created on the sixth day. The concept behind the mark is simple, really. Take it and worship the beast and be able to buy, sell, and eat . . . or starve and be put to death.

It's also worth mentioning that no one in human history has ever caused the whole world to receive such an identifying mark. This is further evidence confirming that the events of Revelation are yet future.

24. Will Antichrist be assassinated?

Revelation 13:3–4 and 17:8 state that the "beast" is killed. Some think this is referring to the death of the Roman Empire, which will come back to life in the last days. But the reemergence of the Roman Empire would not cause the entire world to be in awe and follow after the beast, as Revelation 13:3 states. It makes better interpretive sense to see the beast as referring to a person. In addition, his death is called a "fatal wound" (13:3, 12). The Bible tells us the beast will be slain by "the wound of the sword" (13:14). "Sword" here could be symbolic of death in a general sense, or it could be literal. I see no reason *not* to take it at face value, as personal firearms may very well be prohibited and confiscated under the totalitarian regime of Antichrist. And though the assassin's motivations are unknown, the wound Antichrist suffers is said to be fatal, convincing the entire world he is dead.

The word *slain* used in Revelation 13:3 refers to a violent death, and John used the same word elsewhere in Revelation to describe the death of Jesus (5:6, 9, 12; 13:8).

25. Will Antichrist supernaturally rise from the dead?

The real question here is, does the Antichrist actually die from his wound? Scholars disagree as to whether his resurrection is actual or merely a satanic deception. Those on the side of deception claim only God can raise the dead, and that such a false miracle fits well with the overall delusion of the Tribulation age (2 Thessalonians 2:11). Further, they say that this fake resurrection is yet one more aspect in which this man is "anti-Christ," mimicking or parodying Christ's own resurrection.

At this point in the Tribulation, Revelation 12:12 tells us Satan is infuriated. The last, greatest, and most convincing miracle up his sleeve is to resurrect someone from the dead. Therefore, he saves this trump card to use in his final attempt to be worshiped on earth. No one seriously doubts whether Satan could counterfeit such a miraculous wonder. The question is, *does* he?

Remember, both Jesus and Paul stated that convincing miracles will take place in the last days (Matthew 24:4–5, 11, 24; 2 Thessalonians 2:9; cf. Revelation 13:13–15; 16:13; 19:20). The seven-year Tribulation will be a time of the supernatural, when miracles, signs, and wonders will take place in abundance. And Scripture attributes many of these occurrences to Satan (2 Thessalonians 2:9).

Further, in Revelation, the beast who originally arose out of the sea of humanity (13:1) is now said to "come up out of the abyss," returning to life (13:14; 17:8). This could suggest a passing from the afterlife back into this life, as if Antichrist, following his assassination, went to the abyss (where some demons are kept, and where Satan is later bound). See Revelation 9:1–3; 11:7–8; 17:8; 20:1–3, 7–10.

Scripture calls Satan the "ruler" and "god of this world" (John 12:31; 2 Corinthians 4:4), and this realm is his current domain. And he certainly can counterfeit great miracles in this world. The question is, does his power extend to the afterlife, even for just this one instance? I cannot be 100 percent certain that God, in his sovereignty, would not allow this onetime occurrence to happen. However, I am more convinced of Satan's trickery than I am of his supernatural abilities.

Therefore, my belief is that this resurrection will *probably* be false and staged. I do believe that Satan can perform the actual healing of a wound, as Revelation 13:12 states. And it is also conceivable that Satan has the power to simulate death and a resurrection from the dead. What is not debated is that, whether fake or real, this "miracle" will be convincing enough to win the allegiance and worship of the entire world.

26. Will Antichrist be at Armageddon?

When speaking of Armageddon, we typically think of a single great battle. However, the Bible depicts Armageddon as more of a campaign than a single battle. This military campaign is the culmination of seven years of divine judgments from God on the earth and its inhabitants. More people will die during this seven-year period than during all other conflicts in history combined. From a human perspective, this bloody end is inevitable, as mankind will never achieve world peace on its own. The Bible says that if Jesus Christ did not return, humanity would annihilate one another completely (Matthew 24:22). However, from a scriptural perspective, all this is part of God's grand plan.

"Armageddon" means Mount of Megiddo, and points to a geographical location approximately sixty miles north of Jerusalem. This area was previously the location of some Old Testament battles (Judges 4, 7).

Among Bible scholars and prophecy experts, there is some debate as to the precise order of this battle campaign. The following is a generally accepted sequence and progression:[8]

1. At the sixth bowl judgment, the Euphrates River is dried up, making it possible for the armies from the East to cross it (Revelation 16:12).

2. Three demons performing supernatural signs lure Antichrist's allies to Israel for the purpose of exterminating the Jews once and for all (Revelation 16:12–16).

3. Jerusalem is attacked and falls (Zechariah 12:1–3; 14:2).

4. Antichrist turns his attention south toward the Jewish remnant hiding in or near Petra (Bozrah and/or Edom in Scripture), present-day Jordan (Isaiah 34:6–7; 63:1–5; Joel 3:19; Matthew 24:15–31; Revelation 12:6, 14). Since Jesus previously warned them to flee to the mountains (Matthew 24:16), many believe the ideal place of refuge will be near Bozrah, or Petra, located about eighty miles south of Jerusalem (see Isaiah 63:1–3; Daniel 11:41; Micah 2:12–13). It is believed this mountainous region, containing hundreds of clefts and caves, could protectively shelter around a million people. One-third of the Jews have been hiding there since the midpoint of the tribulation, since the abomination of desolation. The other two-thirds were "cut off" (Zechariah 13:8), presumably slaughtered in Antichrist's previous invasion of Israel and Jerusalem. The Bible says in Revelation 12 that this remnant will be divinely protected by God for three and a half years.

5. Jesus Christ returns from heaven, his feet touching the Mount of Olives, splitting it in two (Zechariah 14:4; Acts 1:10–11).[9]

6. Christ turns to the valley of Jehoshaphat just outside Jerusalem between the Temple Mount and the Mount of Olives, destroying the armies that invaded the city (Joel 3:9–17; Zechariah 12:1–9; 14:3).

7. Jesus then rides to the wilderness (Bozrah) and slays the

armies assembled against the Jewish remnant gathered there. These Jews now likely constitute all of Israel (Romans 11:26). They have come to faith through the ministries of the two witnesses, the 144,000, and other converted Jews. They now presumably call out for their Messiah to deliver them and bring about his kingdom in Israel. Scholars disagree whether or not the Antichrist and the false prophet are present at this particular portion of the battle or whether they are assembled on the plain of Megiddo with the rest of the armies of the world. We do know that Antichrist's armies are spread out for some 200 miles from Megiddo to the north to Bozrah in the south. In any event, Christ slaughters his enemies there and then heads north to Armageddon proper, his sword and robe dripping with the blood of his enemies (Isaiah 34:2–7; 63:1–3; Revelation 19:13–15).

8. The final phase of this Armageddon campaign portrays Jesus on a white horse of victory, leading the armies of heaven behind him. He rides north to slay the remainder of earth's armies gathered at Armageddon (Revelation 19:11–18). This is the most dramatic, climactic, and horrific scene in all of human history. The Bible says the sword of his Word smites his enemies with "the fierce wrath of God, the Almighty" (v. 15). On "His robe and on His thigh He has a name written: 'KING OF KINGS, AND LORD OF LORDS'" (v. 16).

Either here or at Bozrah the Antichrist and false prophet are captured and thrown alive into the lake of fire, which burns with brimstone (2 Thessalonians 2:8; Revelation 19:19–20). This fiery lake now has its first two inhabitants, to be later joined by all the unrighteous at the conclusion of Jesus' thousand-year millennial kingdom on earth. Satan will also be cast there at this time (Revelation 20:1–15).

27. When will Antichrist be revealed?

According to Scripture, Antichrist's identity will not be revealed until after the Rapture (2 Thessalonians 2:1–12). The "day of the Lord," in this context referring to the Tribulation, will not occur until the great apostasy comes and the man of lawlessness is revealed (2:3). Before the Rapture and Tribulation, it becomes an exercise in futility to try to identify the Antichrist. Doing this not only gives ourselves too much credit, but it is evidence of a lack of trust in Scripture, which tells us he won't be made known until later. Further, it also fails to give the Devil his due. Satan is cunning and brilliantly deceptive, and no doubt will do his supernatural best to keep the identity of his chosen man secret until the proper time. And in the event he has several possible candidates he is grooming at various ages and stages of political development, he himself may not even know who Antichrist will be until the Lord rescues his church at the Rapture.

28. Is Antichrist alive today?

Our world is longing for a leader. A savior. A messiah. Unfortunately, it's not the Messiah the Bible describes, but rather a false messiah. And this person could appear at any time. If we are truly living in the last days, then certainly a candidate(s) for Antichrist is also alive. Satan does not know the Rapture's timing, but he is prophetically savvy enough to look around and see what's happening in our world, and how many end-times prophecies are currently in formation. As a result, he's probably getting pretty excited about now. He realizes his time—his seven years of fame—may not be far off.

Again, there may be several potential men who are ripe to become the son of perdition and fulfill this diabolical end-times role. We do know for certain the spirit of the Antichrist is alive today, because the apostle John wrote that it was alive back in the first century, which he described as the "last hour" (1 John 2:18, 22; 4:3; 2 John 7).

So, is *the* Antichrist alive right now? It's very possible, depending of course upon God's preordained time for Jesus' return for his bride. As we look at the character profile for this diabolical man, we do see some of that same deception and wickedness in many known political leaders of our day (arrogant, deceptive, cunning, charismatic, ambitious for more power, etc.). At the same time, it's also very possible Antichrist will not have been known or famous before his ascension to power, but rather will rise out of relative obscurity. Out of the shadows, as it were. We have already seen examples of this in recent history, even in American politics, some even being unexplainably propelled to the highest offices in the land.

29. What is Antichrist waiting on?

According to Scripture, the man of lawlessness will not be revealed until the *restrainer* "is taken out of the way" (2 Thessalonians 2:6–7). I believe this restrainer to be the Holy Spirit's influence through the bride of Christ, the church. In other words, the only thing holding back a complete tsunami of sin in the world is the church, believers in Jesus. You and me. Our current influence here, though at times appearing weak and perhaps futile, is having a greater impact than we may realize. The Source of this influence is the third member of the Godhead, the Holy Spirit. He is sovereignly doing as he wills through the church and in the hearts of the unsaved. And he is restraining the great evil that is coming.

So, if you think people and culture are wicked and godless now, they are nothing compared to what they will be after we have been taken to heaven (1 Timothy 4:1–3; 2 Timothy 3:1–13).

Once we have been raptured, the restraining influence against evil will be removed from planet Earth. The ensuing chaos and panic and the explosion of wickedness will help facilitate the need for a great leader to emerge onto history's shores and bring peace and safety to a planet gone mad.

30. So what? How does knowing all this about Antichrist practically relate to my life now?

No doubt you have wondered this as you've read this book. How do these future truths and events intersect with your life and faith in Christ? It's important to remind ourselves here that some 28 percent of the Bible was prophetic at the time it was written. So over one-fourth of the Scripture is prophecy. Second Timothy 3:16–17 exhorts us that "all Scripture is inspired by God and profitable for teaching, for reproof, for correction, for training in righteousness; so that the man of God may be adequate, equipped for every good work."

It is God's desire for every Christian to study the *entire* Bible, not just the parts that give us warm fuzzy feelings. There are often difficult truths to confront when reading the Bible, particularly those that have to do with ourselves, our sin, our sanctification, and the future of our planet. It is not pleasant to contemplate God's awful judgments that will take place during the Tribulation. But they are real. And they are going to happen exactly as described in prophetic Scripture. And yet these truths are no less real and applicable than the Psalms, the Epistles, or the Beatitudes. So we must engage them for what they are—God's Word, asking the Lord to both teach us *from* them and transform us *with* them.

With that in mind, engaging these prophetic truths concerning Antichrist profits us in several ways:

- They tell us God does have a plan for the ages. Things are not just happening randomly, and the world is not out of control. God has everything under his sovereign direction, and history is progressing precisely toward its appointed end. Knowing this gives us great hope, peace, and security.

- Studying about Antichrist teaches us a lot about the human heart, how wicked we are, and how evil we can, and *will*, become. Seeing the world and how it responds both to God's judgment and to the offer of the gospel during the Tribulation, is a sobering reminder of how deceitful our own hearts can be and how depraved humanity is becoming.

- It shows us how subtle and effective Satan's deceptive schemes are, and that we should never believe a truth or follow a person solely based on *personal need*. No matter how desperate we get or how depressed we become, our circumstances should never dictate the direction of our lives. Even today many weak Christians are falling for false doctrines and following false teachers. The Antichrist is only the ultimate expression of those servants of Satan currently roaming the earth. Presently Satan has many who are serving him, dishing out his devilish lies across the world and inside the church. Therefore, we must be biblically discerning and determined to let Scripture shape our minds.

- Knowing how bad things will get after we are taken by Christ to heaven ought to inspire and motivate us to reach others for Christ now. Whether it's at church, work, school, among friends, neighbors, coworkers, or teammates, God wants to use you as his mouthpiece and hands, spreading the good news of Jesus to your world. The prophetic clock is ticking. And we have no time to waste. You can even use this book as a tool and conversation starter with those you hope to reach.

- The truth about Antichrist clearly demonstrates that God triumphantly wins in the end. Evil cannot, and will not, overcome God's righteousness. Every sin will be punished either on the cross or ultimately in the lake of fire. Therefore, as believers we do not have to be afraid of anything presently happening in our world. Nor should we fear any influence that Satan would send our way. In the heart of Christians, there is also zero fear of the coming Antichrist.

It's also important to realize that even though individuals who place faith in Jesus during the Tribulation will suffer horribly for their faith, that doesn't mean we are exempt from suffering and persecution now. As the hatred of Christians and our Christ continues to grow worldwide, we must be prepared to suffer for his name's sake while standing boldly *against* evil and *for* Jesus and the souls of men.

Lastly, if you're reading this and you are not thoroughly convinced you belong to Jesus Christ, I urge you to call out to him for salvation *right now*. Please don't put off the most important decision you will ever make. Put your complete trust on the Lord Jesus Christ right now and you *will* be saved (Acts 16:31; Romans 10:13). Ask him to forgive your sin and to reign in your heart. Perhaps a prayer like this would express the desire of your heart:

"Lord Jesus, I need you. I admit I am a sinner and deserving of your coming wrath. But I also believe that you love me, and sent Christ to suffer in my place on the cross. Right now, I put my faith in him alone for salvation and the forgiveness of my sins."

Jesus said that being his follower is like being "born again." And just like a newborn child needs nurturing and growth, so do we as well. So, if you trusted Christ for salvation, I encourage you to begin reading God's Word (start with the Gospel of John). Also, find a Bible-teaching church in your area to further feed your new faith.

Being a Christian not only exempts you from the coming Tribulation and Antichrist's wrath, but it also provides you with a guaranteed home in heaven, a new life right now, and, most importantly, a loving relationship with the God and Savior who made you and loves you. Perhaps this reality concerning Antichrist has served to point you toward the *true* Christ!

I trust the story of this book and the biblical section that followed have also inspired you to explore more Bible prophecy concerning the last days. If so, there is no time to waste, so dive in!

When the first-century church contemplated these very truths regarding the last days, their response was to cry out . . .

"Maranatha! . . . Come, Lord Jesus."[10]

And in light of the times in which we live, his return could be very soon.

"He who testifies to these things says, 'Yes, I am coming quickly.' Amen. Come, Lord Jesus" (Revelation 22:20).

ACKNOWLEDGMENTS

I am so grateful to a number of people, all of whom played strategic roles in the creation of this book.

To Joel Kneedler at Thomas Nelson for his innovative vision for this project.

To Janene MacIvor and her editorial team for their expertise in literary detail and accuracy.

To my son Stuart, whose insightful contributions assisted me in character and scene development.

To my millennial focus group, whose feedback was invaluable in keeping my story relevant to the next generation.

I am also deeply thankful for my longtime literary agent, Bill Jensen, whose sage-like wisdom and direction perpetually challenge me to produce my best work.

And finally, to my wife, Beverly. Without her companionship and encouragement, I could never be the man or the writer I am today.

NOTES

Epilogue

1. Tertullian wrote of John's boiling-oil experience at the hands of Rome. See Tertullian, *Prescription Against Heretics*, chap. 36, New Advent website, accessed March 21, 2019, http://www.newadvent.org/fathers/0311.htm.

2. Revelation 6:2; 11:7; 12:17; 13:1–18; 15:2; 16:13; 17:7; 19:20; 20:4, 10.

3. Written around 537 BC, Daniel prophesied a future timeline for the nation of Israel. This timeline would be characterized by 70 groups of 7 years, or 490 years total. The initial 69 groups of 7 comes to 483 years. The clock began ticking with the issuing of the decree to restore and rebuild Jerusalem by Artaxerxes of Persia (Ezra 7:11–28). Fast-forward 483 years from the date of his decree using the Jewish calendar (360 days in a year) and you arrive in AD 32, the very week of Jesus' crucifixion. Daniel 9:25 put it this way: "From the issuing of a decree to restore and rebuild Jerusalem until Messiah the Prince, there will be seven weeks, and sixty-two weeks" (69 weeks). The Messiah is, of course, Jesus. And then God

pressed the pause button, freezing the prophetic clock as it were, leaving a remaining seven years in Daniel's prophetic timeline. Daniel tells us that during this parenthesis of time between the 69th and 70th weeks of his prophecy, several things would happen: (1) the Messiah would be cut off and killed (9:26); (2) the city of Jerusalem would be destroyed [by the Romans] (9:26); and (3) Israel would suffer from that time until Messiah's return.

4. Jeff Kinley, *Wake the Bride: Facing These Last Days with Your Eyes Wide Open* (Eugene, OR: Harvest House, 2015).

5. Saddam Hussein saw himself as a reincarnation, or second coming, of Nebuchadnezzar and began excavating and rebuilding the ancient city of Babylon, from which he would presumably rule, and in which he built a lavish palace.

6. For more on America's relationship and role in Bible prophecy, see Jeff Kinley, *The End of America?: Bible Prophecy and a Country in Crisis* (Eugene, OR: Harvest House, 2017).

7. Mark Hitchcock, *Who Is the Antichrist?: Answering the Question Everyone Is Asking* (Eugene, OR: Harvest House, 2011), 138–40.

8. Some also include in this sequence the fall of Babylon (Isaiah 13:19; Jeremiah 50:9, 13–14, 23–25, 40, 43; 51:31–32).

9. Studies in the earth's crust in this area have led Israeli seismologists to warn that a major quake is expected at any time. See Gman, "The Christ Quake," phpBB: Evidence for God from Science, November 10, 2013, https://discussions.godandscience.org /viewtopic.php?t=38866.

10. 1 Corinthians 16:22; Revelation 22:20. See also Revelation 22:12.

ABOUT THE AUTHOR

Jeff Kinley is the president of Main Thing Ministries, an organization whose mission is to empower people with God's vintage truth. He is the author of thirty-two books and previously served in pastoral ministry for three decades. He hosts the Vintage Truth Podcast, heard twice weekly in more than sixty countries. Jeff speaks around the country on the subject of Bible prophecy. He and his wife, Beverly, live in Arkansas. They have three grown sons. For booking info and more about his ministry, see jeffkinley.com.